ABERDEEN

For crying out loud, she was a freaked-out second-year resident. Gareth had dealt with a lot of freaked-out people in his life—the wounded, the addled, the grieving.

He was good with the freaked-out.

But not like this. Not the way he was thinking.

Hell.

And that was exactly where he was going—*do not pass 'Go', do not collect any money*—because all he could think about now was her mouth.

Kissing it. Giving her a way to *really* forget what was beyond the door.

It was wildly inappropriate.

They were *at work*, for crying out loud.

But her husky, 'Gareth?' reflected the confusion and turmoil stirring unrest inside him.

The look changed on her face as her gaze fixed on his mouth. Her fingers in his shirt seemed to pull him nearer and those freckles were so damn irresistible.

'Oh, screw it,' he muttered, caution falling away like confetti around him as he stepped forward, crowding her back against the door, his body aligning with hers, his palms sliding onto her cheeks as he dropped his head.

Dear Reader

This is the first book I've written where my hero is a nurse. I've been toying with doing it for a long time, but I didn't really have a scenario in my head until recently. Then I saw ex-military triage nurse Gareth in my mind's eye and knew I had my hero.

He's tough and strong and self-reliant, but after thirty doctor/paramedic heroes I thought I'd meet resistance from my editor over Gareth being a nurse and Billie, the heroine, being a doctor. Not the case, however. I was given free rein to bring their story to life and I'm so grateful—because Gareth is just the hero that Billie needs: supportive when required, but challenging her to be the person she *is*...not the person others want her to be. And Billie is just the woman Gareth needs—dragging him back into the world of the living. Helping him live, laugh and love again. Showing him that there is another life for him.

Both of them have pasts that make going ahead with the future complicated. Both of them are facing demons. But that is the beauty and power of love. And for Gareth and Billie falling hard is inevitable.

I hope you enjoy their journey.

Love

Amy

IT HAPPENED ONE NIGHT SHIFT

BY
AMY ANDREWS

First published in Great Britain 2015
by Mills & Boon, an imprint of Harlequin (UK) Limited,
Eton House, 18-24 Paradise Road, Richmond, Surrey, TW9 1SR

© 2015 Amy Andrews

ISBN: 978-0-263-25932-2

Harlequin (UK) Limited's policy is to use papers that are natural,
renewable and recyclable products and made from wood grown in
sustainable forests. The logging and manufacturing processes conform
to the legal environmental regulations of the country of origin.

Printed and bound in Great Britain
by CPI Antony Rowe, Chippenham, Wiltshire

Amy Andrews has always loved writing, and still can't quite believe that she gets to do it for a living. Creating wonderful heroines and gorgeous heroes and telling their stories is an amazing way to pass the day. Sometimes they don't always act as she'd like them to—but then neither do her kids, so she's kind of used to it. Amy lives in the very beautiful Samford Valley, with her husband and aforementioned children, along with six brown chooks and two black dogs. She loves to hear from her readers. Drop her a line at www.amyandrews.com.au

Recent titles by Amy Andrews:

These books are also available in eBook format from www.millsandboon.co.uk

CHAPTER ONE

GARETH STAPLETON DROPPED his head from side to side, stretching out his traps as he kept his eyes on the road.

He was getting too old for this crap.

It had been a long, crazy shift in the emergency room and he needed a beer, a shower and his bed.

Saturday nights in a busy Brisbane ER were chaotic at the best of times but the full moon had added an extra shot of the bizarre to the mix. From now on he was consulting astrological charts when requesting his roster.

He yawned and looked at the dash clock—almost midnight—and was grateful for his shift ending when it had. The waiting room had still been full as he'd clocked off and he didn't envy the night shift having to deal with it all.

Suddenly, the car in front of him—a taxi—swerved slightly into the opposite lane and Gareth's pulse spiked.

What the hell?

Despite only going at the speed limit, he eased back on the accelerator as the taxi corrected itself. Gareth peered into the back windscreen of the car, trying to see what the guy was doing. What was distracting him? Was he texting? Or talking on the phone?

He couldn't tell *what* the driver was doing but at least the taxi appeared to be empty of passengers.

Gareth eased back some more. He may only be driving a twenty-year-old rust box but he had no desire to be collateral damage due to this clown's inattention. Luckily they were on a long, straight section of road linking two outer suburbs so there were no houses, no cars parked on either side, just trees and bushland.

The taxi wobbled all over the lane again and Gareth's stomach tightened as a set of oncoming headlights suddenly winked in the distance. His fingers gripped the steering-wheel a little firmer as a sense of foreboding settled over him.

Gareth's sense of foreboding had served him well over the years—particularly in the Middle East—and it wasn't going to be disappointed tonight.

He watched in horror as the taxi swerved suddenly again into the path of the oncoming car. Gareth hit his horn but it was futile, the crash playing out in front of him in slow motion.

The driver of the other car slammed on the brakes, swerving to avoid what Gareth could have sworn was certain collision. He waited for the crash and the sound of crunching metal but, thankfully, it never came. The taxi narrowly missed the other car, careening off the road and smashing into a tree.

But now the oncoming car was in his lane and Gareth had to apply his brakes to prevent them crashing. Luckily the other driver had the good sense to swerve back into his own lane and they both came to a halt almost level with each other on their own sides of the road.

Gareth, his heart pistoning like a jackhammer, automatically reached for his glove box and pulled out a bunch of gloves from a box he always kept there. He ripped his seat belt off and pushed open his door.

'Are you okay, mate?' he asked as he leapt out, his fingers already reaching for the mobile phone in his pocket as he mentally triaged the scene.

He wrenched open the door of the other car, noticing absently it was a sleek-looking two-seater, to find a pair of huge brown eyes, heavily kohled and fringed with sooty eyelashes, blinking back at him. A scarlet mouth formed a surprised-looking O.

A woman.

'I'm…I'm fine.' She nodded, looking dazed.

Gareth wasn't entirely sure. She appeared uninjured but she looked like she might be in shock. 'Can you move? How's your neck?' he asked.

She nodded again, undoing her seat belt. 'It's fine. I'm fine.' She swung her legs out of the car.

'Don't move,' he ordered. 'Stay there.' The last thing he needed was a casualty wandering around the scene. 'I'm Gareth, what's your name?'

'Billie.'

Gareth acknowledged the unusual name on a superficial level only. 'I'm going to check out the taxi driver. You stay here, okay, Billie?'

She blinked up at him and nodded. 'Okay.'

Satisfied he'd secured her co-operation, Gareth, already dialling triple zero, headed for the smashed-up taxi.

It took a minute for Billie to come out of the fog of the moment and get her bearings. She'd told Gareth—at least that was what she thought he'd said his name was—she was okay. Everything had happened so fast. But a quick mental check of her body confirmed it.

She was shaking like a leaf but she wasn't injured.

And she was a doctor. She shouldn't be sitting in her car like an invalid—she should be helping.

What on earth had caused the taxi to veer right into her path? Was the driver drunk? Or was it something medical? A hypo? A seizure?

She reached across to her glove box and pulled out a pair of gloves from the box she always kept there, her heart beating furiously, mentally preparing herself for potential gore. Being squeamish was not something that boded well for a doctor but it was something she'd never been able to conquer.

She'd learned to control it—just.

She exited her car, yanking the boot lever on the way out, rounding the vehicle and pulling out a briefcase that contained a well-stocked first-aid kit. Then she took a deep breath and in her ridiculous heels and three-quarter-length cocktail dress she made her way over to the crashed car and Gareth.

Gareth looked up from his ministrations as Billie approached. 'I thought I'd told you to stay put,' he said, whipping off his fleecy hoody, not even feeling the cool air. His only priority was getting the driver, who wasn't breathing and had no pulse, out of the car.

'I'm fine. And I'm a doctor so I figured I could help.'

Gareth was momentarily thrown by the information but he didn't have time to question her credentials. She was already wearing a pair of hospital-issue gloves that *he* hadn't given her, so she was at least prepared.

And the driver's lips were turning from dusky to blue.

He needed oxygen and a defib. Neither of which they had.

All the driver had was them, until the ambulance got there.

'I'm an ER nurse,' Gareth said, rolling his hoody into a tube shape then carefully wrapping it around the man's neck, fashioning a crude soft collar to give him some C-spine protection when they pulled him out.

'Ambulance is ten minutes away. He's in cardiac arrest. Thankfully he's not trapped. Help me get him out and we'll start CPR. I'll grab his top half,' Gareth said.

Aided by the light from the full moon blasting down on them, they had the driver lying on the dew-damp grass in less than thirty seconds. 'You maintain the airway,' Gareth said, falling back on protocols ingrained in him during twenty years in the field. 'I'll start compressions.'

Billie nodded, swallowing hard as the metallic smell from the blood running down the driver's face from a deep laceration on his forehead assaulted her senses. It had already congealed in places and her belly turned at the sight, threatening to eject the three-course meal she'd indulged in earlier.

She turned away briskly, sucking air slowly into her lungs. In through her nose, out through her mouth, concentrating on the cold damp ground already seeping through the gauzy fabric of her dress to her knees rather than the blood. She was about to start her ER rotation—she had to get used to this.

She opened the briefcase and pulled out her pocket mask.

Gareth kicked up an eyebrow as she positioned herself, a knee either side of the guy's head, and held the mask efficiently in place over the driver's mouth and nose.

'Very handy,' he said, noting her perfect jaw grasp and hand placement. 'Don't suppose you have a defib in there by any chance?'

Billie gave a half-laugh. 'Sadly, no.' Because they both knew that's what this man needed.

She leaned down to blow several times into the mouthpiece. Her artfully curled hair fell forward and she quickly pushed them behind her ears as the mask threatened to slip. The mix of sweat and blood on the driver's face worked against her and Billie had to fight back a gag as the smell invaded her nostrils.

If she just shut her eyes and concentrated on the flow of air, the rhythm of her delivery, mentally counted the breaths, she might just get through this without disgracing herself.

'What do you reckon, heart attack?' Gareth asked after he'd checked for a pulse two minutes in.

Billie, concentrating deeply, opened her eyes at the sudden intrusion. Rivulets of dried blood stared back at her and she quickly shut them again. 'Probably,' she said between breaths. 'Something caused him to veer off the road like that and he feels pretty clammy. Only he looks young, though. Fit too.'

Gareth agreed, his arms already feeling the effort of prolonged compressions. The man didn't look much older than himself. ''Bout forty, I reckon.'

Billie nodded. 'Too young to die.'

He grunted and Billie wondered if he was thinking the same thing she was. The taxi driver probably *was* going to die. The statistics for out-of-hospital cardiac arrests were grim. Even for young, fit people. This man needed so much more than they could give him here on the roadside.

They fell silent again as they continued to give a complete stranger, who had nearly wiped both of them out tonight, a chance at life.

'Come on, mate,' Gareth said, as he checked the pulse for the third time and went back to compressions. 'Cut us some slack here.'

A minute later, the silence was pierced by the first low wails of a siren. 'Yes,' Gareth muttered. 'Hold on, mate. The cavalry's nearly here.'

In another minute two ambulances—one with an intensive care paramedic—pulled up, followed closely by a police car. A minute after that a fire engine joined the fray. Reinforcements surrounded them, artificial light suddenly flooding the scene, Billie and Gareth continued their CPR as Gareth gave an impressive rapid-fire handover.

'Keep managing the airway,' the female intensive care paramedic instructed Billie, after Gareth had informed her of their medical credentials. She handed Billie a proper resus set—complete with peep valve and oxygen supply. 'You okay to intubate?'

Billie nodded. She could. As a second-year resident she'd done it before but not a lot. And then there was the blood.

She took another deep, steadying breath.

Gareth continued compressions as one of the advanced care paramedics slapped on some defib pads and the other tried to establish IV access.

In the background several firemen dealt with the car, some set up a road block with the police while others directed a newly arrived tow truck to one side.

The automatic defibrillator warned everyone to move away from the patient as it advised a shock.

'Stand clear,' the paramedic called, and everyone dropped what they were doing and moved well back.

A series of shocks was delivered, to no avail, and everyone resumed their positions. IV access was gained and emergency drugs were delivered. Billie successfully intubated as Gareth continued with cardiac massage. Two minutes later the defibrillator recommended another shock and everyone moved away again.

The driver's chest arched. 'We've got a rhythm,' the paramedic announced.

Gareth reached over and felt for the carotid. 'Yep,' he agreed. 'I have a pulse.'

'Okay, let's get him loaded and go.'

Billie reached for the bag to resume respiratory support on the still unconscious patient but the intensive care paramedic crouched beside Billie said, 'Would you like me to take over?'

Billie looked at her, startled. She'd been concentrating so hard on not losing her stomach contents she'd shut everything out other than the whoosh of her own breath. But the airway was secure and they had a pulse. She could easily hand over to a professional who had way more experience dealing with these situations.

Not to mention the fact that now the emergency was under control her hands were shaking, her teeth were chattering and she was shivering with the cold.

And her knees were killing her.

She looked down at her gloves. They were streaked with blood and another wave of nausea welled inside her.

Billie handed the bag over and then suddenly warm hands were lifting her up onto her shaking legs, supporting her as her numb knees threatened to buckle. A blanket was thrown around her shoulders and she huddled into its warmth as she was shepherded in the direction of her car.

'Are you okay?'

Billie glanced towards the deep voice, surprised to find herself looking at Gareth. He was tall and broad and looked warm and inviting and she felt so cold. She had the strangest urge to walk into his arms.

'I'm fine,' she said, gripping the blanket tighter around her shoulders, looking down at where her gloved hands held the edges of the blanket together.

Dried blood stared back at her. The nausea she'd been valiantly trying to keep at bay hit her in a rush.

And right there, dressed to the nines in front of Gareth and a dozen emergency personnel, she bent over and threw up her fancy, two-hundred-dollar, three-course meal on the side of the road.

CHAPTER TWO

BILLIE WAS THANKFUL as she talked to the police a few minutes later she'd never have to see anyone here ever again. She doubted if any of these seasoned veterans blinked an eye at someone barfing at the scene of an accident and they'd all been very understanding but she was *the doctor,* for crying out loud.

People looked to her to be the calm, in-control one. To take bloodied accident victims in her stride. She was *supposed* to be able to hold herself together.

Not throw up at the sight of blood and gore.

Billie wondered anew how she was going to cope in the emergency room for the next six months. For the rest of her life, for that matter, given that emergency medicine was her chosen career path.

Mostly because it was high-flying enough to assuage parental and family expectations without being surgical. The Ashworth-Keyes of the world were *all* surgeons. Choosing a non-surgical specialty was *not* an option.

Unless it carried the same kind of kudos. As emergency medicine, apparently, did.

And at least this way Billie knew she'd still be able to treat the things that interested her most. Raw and messy were not her cup of tea but infections and diseases, the run-of-the-mill medical problems that were seen in GP practices across the country every day were.

But Ashworth-Keyes' were *not* GPs.

And Billie was carrying a double load of expectation.

She glanced across at Gareth, who was looking relaxed and assured amidst a tableau of clashing lights. The milky phosphorescence of the moon, the glow of fluorescent safety striping on multiple uniforms and the garish strobing of red, blue and amber. He didn't seem to be affected by any of it, his deep, steady voice carrying towards her on the cool night air as he relayed the details of the accident to a police officer.

Billie cringed as she recalled how he'd held her hair back and rubbed between her shoulders blades as she'd hurled up everything in her stomach. Then had sourced some water for her to rinse her mouth out and offered her a mint.

It seemed like he'd done it before. But, then, she supposed, an ER nurse probably *had* done it a thousand times.

Still...why did she have to go and disgrace herself in front of possibly the most good-looking man she'd seen in a very long time?

She'd noticed it subliminally while they'd been performing CPR but she'd had too much else going on, what with holding someone's life in the balance and trying not to vomit, to give her thoughts free rein.

But she didn't now.

And she let them run wild as she too answered a policeman's questions.

Billie supposed a lot of her friends wouldn't classify Gareth as good looking purely because of his age. The grey whiskers putting some salt into the sexy growth of stubble at his jaw and the small lines around his eyes that crinkled a little as he smiled told her he had to be in his late thirties, early forties.

But, then, she'd always preferred older men.

She found maturity sexy. She liked the way, by and large, older men were content in their skins and didn't feel the need to hem a woman in to validate themselves. The easy way they spoke and the way they carried their bodies and wore their experience on their faces and were comfortable with that. She liked the way so many of them didn't seem like they had anything to prove.

She liked how Gareth embodied that. Even standing in the middle of an accident scene he looked at ease.

Gareth laughed at something the policeman said and she watched as he raked a piece of hair back that had flopped forward. She liked his hair. It was wavy and a little long at the back, brushing his collar, and he wore it swept back where it fell in neat rippled rows.

She'd noticed, as they'd tried to save the driver's life, it was dark with some streaks of grey, like his whiskers.

And she liked that too.

His arm dropped back down by his side and her gaze drifted to his biceps. She'd noticed those biceps as well while they'd been working on their man. How could she not have? Every time she'd opened her eyes there they'd been, contracting and releasing with each downward compression.

Firm and taut. Barely covered—*barely constrained*—by his T-shirt.

Billie shivered. She wasn't sure if it was from the power of his biceps alone or the fact he was wandering around on a winter's night with just a T-shirt covering his chest.

Why hadn't someone given him a blanket?

Although, to be fair, he did look a lot more appropriately dressed for a roadside emergency than she did. His jeans looked snug and warm, encasing long, lean legs, and he *had* been wearing a fleecy hoody.

It sure beat a nine-hundred-dollar dress and a pair of strappy designer shoes.

He looked up then, pointing in the direction she'd been driving, and their gazes met. He nodded at her briefly, before returning his attention to the police officer, and she found herself nodding back.

Yep, Billie acknowledged—Gareth was one helluva good-looking man. In fact, he ticked all her boxes. And if she was up for a fling or available for dating in the hectic morass of a resident's life then he'd be exactly her type. But there was absolutely no hope for them now.

The man had held her hair back while she'd vomited.

She cringed again. If she ever saw him again it would be too soon.

Gareth was acutely aware of Billie's gaze as he answered the police officer's questions. It seemed to beam through the cold air like an invisible laser, hot and direct, hitting him fair in the chest, diffusing heat and awareness to every millimetre of his body.

It made her hard to ignore.

Of course, the fact she was sparkling like one of those movie vampires also made her hard to ignore.

The gauzy skirt of her black dress shimmered with hundreds of what looked like crystal beads. Who knew, maybe they were diamonds? The dress certainly didn't look cheap. But they caught the multitude of lights strobing across the scene, refracting them like individual disco balls.

As if the dress and the petite figure beneath needed to draw any more attention to itself. Every man here, from the fireman to the paramedics, the police to the tow-truck driver, was sure as hell taking a moment to appreciate it.

Their attention irritated him. And the fact that it did irritated him even more. She was a stranger and they were at an accident scene, for crying out loud!

But it didn't stop him from going over to her when the police officer was done. He told himself it was to check she was feeling okay now but the dress was weirdly mesmerising and he would have gone to her even if she'd not conveniently vomited twenty minutes ago.

She had her back to him but, as if she'd sensed him approaching, she turned as he neared. Her loose reddish-brown hair flowed silkily around her shoulders, her hair curling in long ringlets around her face. Huge gold hoop earrings he'd noticed earlier as she'd administered the kiss of life swung in her lobes, giving her a little bit of gypsy.

He smiled as he drew closer. She seemed to hesitate for a moment then reciprocated, her scarlet lipstick having worn off from her earlier ministrations.

'You sure know how to dress for a little unscheduled road-side assistance,' he said, as he drew to a halt in front of her.

Billie blinked, surprised by his opening line for a moment, and then she looked down at herself and laughed. 'Oh, yes, sorry,' she said, although she had absolutely no idea why she was apologising for her attire. 'I've just come from a gala reception.'

This close his biceps were even more impressive and Billie had to grip the blanket hard to stop from reaching her hands out and running her palms over them. She wondered if they'd feel as firm and warm as they looked.

'Aren't you cold?' she asked, engaging her mouth before her brain as she dragged her gaze back to his face.

He did a smile-shrug combo and Billie's stomach did a little flip-flop combo in response. 'I'm fine,' he dismissed.

Billie grimaced. Where had she heard that already tonight? 'I really am very sorry about earlier.'

'Yeah.' He grinned. His whole face crinkled and Billie lost her breath as his sexiness increased tenfold. 'You've already said so. Three times.'

She blushed. 'I know but…I think I may have splashed your shoes.'

Gareth looked down at his shoes. 'They've seen far worse, trust me.'

'Not exactly the impression I like to give people I've just met.'

Gareth shrugged. She needn't have been worried about her impression on him—he doubted he was going to forget her in a long time, and it had nothing to do with his shoes and everything to do with how good she looked in those gold hoops and sparkly dress.

And if he'd been up for some flirting and some let's-see-
where-this-goes fun he might just have assured her out loud.
He might just have suggested they try for a second impression. But *hooking up* really wasn't his thing.

Hooking up at an accident scene even less so.

'We haven't exactly met properly, have we? I mean, not
formally.' He held out his hand. 'I'm Gareth Stapleton. Very
pleased to make your acquaintance—despite the circumstances.'

Billie slipped her hand into his and even though she'd
expected to feel something, the rush of warmth up her arm
took her by surprise. She shook his hand absently, staring
at their clasped fingers, pleased for the blanket around her
torso as the warmth rushed all the way to her nipples, prick-
ling them to attention.

Gareth smiled as Billie's gaze snagged on their joined
hands. Not that he could blame her. If she felt the connection
as strongly as he did then they were both in trouble.

Just as well they wouldn't be seeing each other again
after tonight. Resisting her in this situation was sensible and
right. But if there was repeated exposure? That could wear
a man down.

Sensible and right could be easily eroded.

'And you're Billie?' he prompted, withdrawing his hand.
'Billie…?'

Billie dragged her gaze away from their broken grip, up
his broad chest and deliciously whiskery neck and onto his
face, his spare cheekbones glowing alternately red and blue
from the lights behind him.

What were they talking about? Oh, yes, formal introduc-
tions. 'Ashworth-Keyes,' she said automatically. 'Although if
you want *formal* formal then it's *Willamina* Ashworth-Keyes.'

Gareth quirked an eyebrow as a little itch started at the
back of his brain. 'Your first name is *Willamina*?'

Billie rolled her eyes. 'Yes,' she said, placing her hand on
her hip. 'What about it?'

Gareth held up his hands in surrender. 'Nothing. Just kind of sounds like somebody's…spinster great-aunt.'

Billie frowned, unfortunately agreeing. Which was why she'd carried over her childhood pet name into adulthood.

'Not that there's anything *remotely* spinsterish or great-auntish about you,' he hastened to add. The last thing he wanted to do was insult her. The *very* last thing. 'Or,' he added as her frowned deepened, 'that there's anything wrong with that anyway.'

This woman made him tongue-tied.

How long had it been since he'd felt this gauche? Like some horny fifteen-year-old who couldn't even speak to the cool, pretty girl because he had a hard-on the size of a house.

Not that he had a hard-on. Not right now anyway. Or probably ever again if this excruciatingly awkward scene replayed in his head as often as he figured it would.

Billie's breath caught at Gareth's sudden lack of finesse. It made her feel as if she wasn't the only one thrown by this rather bizarre thing that had flared between them.

And she'd liked his emphasis on *remotely*.

She laughed to ease the strange tension that had spiked between them. 'Only my parents call me Willamina,' she said. 'And generally only if I'm in trouble.'

'And are you often in trouble?'

Gareth realised the words might have come across as flirty, so he kept his face serious.

Billie felt absurdly like laughing at such a preposterous notion. Her? In trouble? 'No. Not me. *Never me.*' That had been her sister's job. 'No, I'm the peacekeeper in the family.'

Gareth frowned at the sudden gloom in her eyes. The conversation had swung from light to awkward to serious. It seemed she wasn't too keen on the mantle of family good girl and suddenly a seductive voice was whispering they could find some trouble together.

Thankfully the little itch at the back of his brain finally came into sharp focus, obliterating the voice completely.

'Wait...' He narrowed his eyes. 'Ashworth-Keyes? As in Charles and Alisha Ashworth-Keyes, eminent cardiothoracic surgeons?'

Billie nodded. *Sprung.* 'The very same.'

'Your parents?' She nodded and he whistled. Everyone who was anyone in the medical profession in Brisbane knew of the Ashworth-Keyes surgical dynasty. 'That's some pedigree you've got going on there.'

'Yes. Lucky me,' she said derisively.

'You...don't get on?'

Billie sighed. 'No, it's not that. I'm just...not really like them, you know?'

He quirked an eyebrow. 'How so?'

'Well, I'm no surgeon, that's for sure. I'm a little too squeamish for that.'

Gareth surprised himself by laughing at the understatement but he couldn't help himself. 'Really?' he asked, looking down at his shoes. 'You hide it well.'

Billie shot him a cross look but soon joined him in his laughter.

'And?' he asked. 'What else?'

What else? Being a surgeon was all that mattered in the Ashworth-Keyes household. 'It's...complicated.'

Gareth nodded. Fair enough. Complicated he understood. It really wasn't any of his business anyway. 'So what field is the next Ashworth-Keyes going to specialise in? Clearly something...anything that doesn't involve the letting of blood? Dermatology? Radiology? Maybe...pathology?'

Billie shook her head. 'Emergency medicine,' she said. Even saying it depressed the hell out of her.

Gareth blinked. 'Really?' Surely Billie understood the squeamish factor could get pretty high in an ER?

'Yep,' she confirmed, sounding about as enthusiastic as he usually did just prior to starting a night shift. 'I'm starting my six-month emergency rotation at St Luke's ER next week in fact.'

Gareth held his breath. 'St Luke's?'

'Yes.

Crap. 'Ah.'

She frowned at him in that way he'd already grown way too fond of. 'What?'

'That's where I work.'

'You…work at St Luke's?'

He nodded. 'In the ER.'

'So we'll be…working together,' she murmured.

'Yup.'

And he hoped like hell she didn't look as good in a pair of scrubs as she did in a black sparkly dress or *sensible* and *right* were going to be toast.

CHAPTER THREE

BILLIE'S FIRST DAY at St Luke's wasn't as bad as she'd thought. Gareth wasn't there and she was able to slip into the groove of the department during daytime hours when there were a lot of senior staff around to have her back and take on the more raw and challenging cases.

She was content to take the nuisance admissions that everybody grumbled about. The patients that should be at their GPs' but had decided to save their hip pockets and clutter up the public waiting room instead.

Billie really didn't mind. It was satisfying work and she took to it like a duck to water. Her previous six months had been her medical rotation and she'd thrived there as well, treating a variety of cases from the humdrum to the interesting.

It was Thursday she wasn't looking forward to. Thursday was the start of three night shifts and from nine until eight the next morning there were just three residents—her and two others—and a registrar, dealing with whatever came through the doors.

Actually, Thursday night probably wasn't going to be so bad. It was Friday and Saturday night that had her really worried. The city bars would be open and the thought of having to deal with the product of too much booze and testosterone wasn't a welcome one.

There would be blood.

Of that she was sure.

Nine o'clock Thursday night rocked around quicker than Billie liked and she walked into St Luke's ER with a sense of foreboding.

Her hands shook as she changed into a set of scrubs in the female change room. '*St. Luke's ER*' was embroidered on the pocket in case Billie needed any further reminders that she was exactly where she didn't want to be. Jen, the other resident who had also started her rotation on the same day, chatted away excitedly and Billie let her run on, nodding and making appropriate one-word comments in the right places.

At least it was a distraction.

Thankfully, though, by the time the night team had taken handover at the central work station from the day team, Billie was feeling a little more relaxed.

Things were reasonably quiet. The resus bays were empty and only a handful of patients were in varying stages of being assessed, most of them with medical complaints that didn't involve any level of gore.

Billie knew she could handle that with one hand tied behind her back. In fact, she was looking forward to it.

A nurse cruised by and Helen, the registrar, introduced the three new residents. 'Who's on the night shift, Chrissy, do you know?'

'Gareth,' she said.

Billie's pulse leapt at his name. Helen smiled. 'Excellent.'

Chrissy rolled her eyes. 'Yeah, yeah,' she joked. 'Everyone loves Gareth.'

Helen laughed. 'He's highly experienced,' she said, feigning affront.

'Sure,' Chrissy teased. 'And those blue eyes have nothing at all to do with it.'

'Blue eyes? I hadn't noticed.' Helen shrugged nonchalantly.

'Who's Gareth?' Barry, the other new resident, asked as Chrissy left to attend to a buzzer.

'Brilliant nurse. Ex-military. Used to be in charge around here. Not sure why he was demoted...think there was some kind of incident. But, anyway, he's very experienced.'

'Ex-military?' Billie's voice sounded an octave or two higher than she would have liked but no one seemed to notice. No wonder Gareth had taken charge of the scene so expertly on Saturday night.

'Apparently,' Helen said. 'Served in MASH units all over. The Middle East most recently, I think. Exceptionally cool and efficient in an emergency.'

Billie nodded. She knew all about that coolness and efficiency.

'Also...' Helen smiled '...kind of easy on the eyes.'

She nodded again. Oh, yes. Billie definitely knew how easy he was on the eyes.

'Right,' Helen said. 'Let's get to it. Let's see if we can't whittle these patients down and have us a quiet night.'

A quiet night sounded just fine to Billie as she picked up a chart and tried not to think about seeing Gareth again in less than two hours.

Gareth came upon Billie just after midnight. He'd known, since he'd checked out the residents' roster, they'd be working together for these next three nights.

And had thought about little else since.

She had her stethoscope in her ears and was listening to the chest of an elderly woman in cubicle three when he peeled the curtain back. She didn't hear him and he stood by the curtain opening, waiting for her to finish, more than content to observe and wait patiently.

She looked *very* different tonight from the last time he'd seen her. Her hair was swept back in a no-nonsense ponytail. The long curling spirals were not falling artfully around her face as they had on Saturday night but were ruthlessly hauled back into the ponytail, giving her hair a sleek, smooth finish. Her earlobes were unadorned, her face free of make-up.

And…*yup*. He'd known it. Even from a side view she rocked a pair of scrubs.

'Well, you've certainly got a rattle on there, Mrs Gordon,' Billie said, as she pulled the stethoscope out of her ears and slung it around her neck.

'Oh, yes, dear,' the elderly patient agreed. Billie was concerned about her flushed face and poor skin turgor. 'I do feel quite poorly.'

'I don't doubt it,' Billie clucked. 'Your X-ray is quite impressive. I think we need to get you admitted and pop in a drip. We can get you rehydrated and give you some antibiotics for that lung infection.'

'Oh, I don't want you to trouble yourself,' Mrs Gordon said.

Billie smiled at her patient. The seventy-three-year-old, whose granddaughter had insisted was usually the life of the party, looked quite frail. She slipped her hand on top of the older, wrinkled one and gave it a squeeze. It felt hot and dry too.

'It's no trouble Mrs Gordon. That's what I'm here for.'

Mrs Gordon smiled back, patting Billie's hand. 'Well, that's lovely of you,' she murmured. 'But I think that young man wants to talk to you, my dear.'

Billie looked over her shoulder to find Gareth standing in a break in the curtain. He did that smile-shrug combo again and her belly flip-flopped once more. 'Hi,' she said.

'Hey,' Gareth murmured, noticing absently the cute sprinkle of freckles across the bridge of her nose and the clear gloss on her lips. Her mouth wasn't the lush scarlet temptation it had been on the weekend but its honeyed glaze drew his eyes anyway.

'Thought I'd pop in and see how you were getting on.'

'Oh…I'm fine…good…thank you.' She sounded breathy and disjointed and mentally pulled herself together. 'Just going to place an IV here and get Mrs Gordon…' she looked down at her patient and smiled '…admitted.'

Gareth nodded. She looked cool and confident in her scrubs, a far cry from the woman who'd admitted to being squeamish after losing her dinner in front of him on Saturday night. He had to give her marks for bravado.

'Do you want me to insert it?'

Billie frowned, perplexed for a moment before realising what he meant. He thought she'd baulk at inserting a cannula? Resident bread and butter?

God, just how flaky had she come across at the accident?

Another thought crossed her mind. He hadn't told anyone in the department about what had happened the other night, had he? About how she'd reacted afterwards?

He wouldn't have, surely?

She looked across at him and Helen was right, his blue scrubs set off the blue of his eyes to absolute perfection. The temptation to get lost in them was startlingly strong but she needed him to realise they weren't on the roadside any more. This was her job and she *could* do it.

She'd been dealing with her *delicate constitution,* as her father had so disparagingly called it, for a lot of years. Yes, it presented its challenges in this environment but she didn't need him to hold her hand.

'Do you think we could talk?' she asked him, before turning and patting her patient's hand. 'I'll be right back, Mrs Gordon. I just need to get some equipment.'

Gareth figured he'd overstepped the mark as he followed the business like swing of her ponytail. But he *had* seen her visibly pale at the sight of the blood running down the taxi driver's face on Saturday night. Had held her hair back while she'd vomited then listened to her squeamishness confession.

Was it wrong to feel protective of her? To want to alleviate the potential for more incidents when he was free and more than capable of doing the procedure himself?

Her back was ramrod straight and her stride brisk as she

yanked open the staffroom door. He followed her inside and Billie turned on him as soon as the door shut behind them.

'What are you doing?' she asked.

Gareth quirked an eyebrow at her. 'Trying to help? I wasn't sure if putting in IVs made you feel faint or nauseated and...' he shrugged '...I was free.'

She shoved her hands on her hips and Gareth noticed for the first time how short she was in her sensible work flats. He seemed to have a good foot on her. Just how high *had* those heels been the other night?

'Would you have offered to do anyone else's?' she demanded.

Gareth folded his arms. 'If I knew it made them squeamish, of course,' he said.

'Putting in an IV *does not* make me squeamish,' she snapped.

'Well, excuse me for trying to be nice,' he snapped back. 'You looked like you had a major issue with blood on Saturday night.'

Billie blinked at his testy comeback. She looked down at her hands. They were clenched hard at her sides and the unreasonable urge to pummel them against his chest beat like insects wings inside her head.

She shook her head. What was she doing? She was acting like a shrew. She took a deep breath and slowly unclenched her hands.

'I can put in an IV,' she sighed. 'I can draw blood, watch it flow into a tube, no problems. It's not *blood* that makes me squeamish, it's blood pouring out where it shouldn't be. It's the gore. The messy rawness. The missing bits and the... jagged edges. The...gaping wounds. That's what I find hard to handle. That's when it gets to me.'

Gareth nodded, pleased for the clarification. The ER was going to be a rough rotation for her. He took a couple of paces towards her, stopping an arm's length away.

'There's a lot of messy rawness here,' he said gently.

'I know,' Billie said. *Boy, did she know.* 'But that's the way it is and I don't want you protecting me from all of it, Gareth. I'm training to be an emergency physician. I'm just going to have to get used to it.'

She watched as his brow crinkled and the lines around his eyes followed suit. 'Why?' he asked. 'Surely this isn't the right speciality for you?'

Billie gave a half snort, half laugh. That *was* the million-dollar question. But despite feeling remarkably at ease with him, there were some things she wasn't prepared to admit to *anybody*.

'Well, yes…and there's a very long, very complicated answer to that question, which I do not have time to tell you right now.' *Or ever.* 'Not with Mrs Gordon waiting.'

Gareth nodded. He knew when he was being fobbed off but, given that she barely knew him, she certainly didn't owe him any explanations. And probably the less involved he was in her stuff the better.

He was a forty-year-old man who didn't need any more *complicated* in his life.

No matter what package it came wrapped in.

He'd had enough of it to last a lifetime.

'Okay, then,' he said, turning to go. 'Just yell if I can help you with anything.'

He had his hand on the doorknob when her tentative enquiry stopped him dead in his tracks.

'You didn't…you haven't told anyone about the other night, about what I…?' He caught her nervous swallow as he faced her. 'About how I reacted? Please…don't…'

Gareth regarded her seriously. If she'd known him better he would have given her a *what-do-you-think?* look. But she didn't, he reminded himself. It just *felt* like they'd known each other longer because of the connection they'd made less than a week ago.

It was hard to think of her as a stranger even though the reality was they barely knew each other.

He shook his head. 'I don't tell tales out of school, Billie,' he said.

He didn't kiss and tell either.

The sudden unwarranted thought slapped him in the face, resulting in temporary brain malfunction.

What the hell?

Pull it together, man. Totally inappropriate. Totally not cool.

But the truth was, as he busied himself with opening the door and getting as far away from her as possible, he'd thought about kissing Billie *a lot* these last few days.

And it had been a very long time since he'd *wanted* to kiss anyone.

CHAPTER FOUR

FIVE HOURS LATER, Gareth knew he was going to have to put Billie's I-don't-want-you-protecting-me convictions to the test. He had a head laceration that needed suturing and everyone else was busy. He could leave it until Barry was free but, with the Royal Brisbane going on diversion, a lot of their cases were coming to St Luke's and things had suddenly gone a little crazy.

They needed the bed asap.

If he'd still been in the army he would have just done the stupid thing himself. But civilian nursing placed certain restrictions on his practice.

Earlier Billie had demanded to know if he'd have given another doctor the kid-glove treatment he'd afforded her over the IV and had insisted that he not do the same to her.

Would he given any other doctor a pass on the head lac?

No. He would not.

Gareth took a deep breath and twitched the curtains to cubicle eight open. Billie looked up from the patient she was talking to. 'I need a head lac sutured in cubicle two,' he said, his tone brisk and businesslike. 'You just about done here?'

She looked startled at his announcement but he admired her quick affirmative response. 'Five minutes?' she said, only the bob of her throat betraying her nervousness.

He nodded. 'I'll set up.'

But then Brett, the triage admin officer, distracted him

with a charting issue and it was ten minutes before he headed
back to the drunk teenager with the banged-up forehead. He
noticed Billie disappearing behind the curtain and cursed
under his breath, hurrying to catch her up.

He hadn't cleaned the wound yet and the patient looked
pretty gruesome.

When he joined her behind the curtain seconds later,
Billie was staring down at the matted mess of clotted blood
and hair that he'd left covered temporarily with a green surgical towel. 'I'm sorry,' he apologised. 'I haven't had a chance
to clean it up yet.'

She dragged her eyes away from the messy laceration and
looked at him, her freckles suddenly emphasised by her pallor, her nostrils flaring as she sucked in air. 'I'll be…right
back,' she said.

She brushed past him on her way out and Gareth shut his
eyes briefly. *Great.* He glanced at the sleeping patient, snor-
ing drunkenly and oblivious to the turmoil his stupid split
head had just caused.

Gareth followed her, taking a guess that she'd headed for
the staffroom again. The door was shut when he reached
it. He turned the handle but it was locked. 'Billie,' he said,
keeping his voice low, 'it's me, open up.'

The lock turned and the door opened a crack and Gareth
slipped into the room. She was just on the other side and
her back pushed the door shut again as she leaned against it.

Billie looked up at him, the swimmy sensation in her
head and the nausea clearing. 'I'm fine,' she dismissed, taking deep, even steady breaths.

'I'm sorry. I had every intention of cleaning it up…so it
looked better.'

Billie nodded. 'It's okay. I'm fine,' she repeated. 'I just
need a moment.'

Gareth nodded as he watched her suck air in and out
through pursed lips. She lifted her hand to smooth her hair
and he couldn't help but notice how alarmingly it shook.

She didn't look okay to him.

'You look kind of freaked out,' he said. 'Do you need a paper bag to blow into? Are your fingers tingly?'

She glared at him. 'I'm not having a panic attack. I just wasn't expecting…that. I'm better if I'm mentally prepared. But I'll be fine.' She turned those big brown eyes on him. 'Just give me a moment, okay?'

'Okay.'

She nodded again and he noticed tears swim in her eyes. Clearly she was disappointed in herself, in not being able to master her affliction.

Gareth shoved a hand through his hair, feeling helpless as she struggled for control. 'Try not to think about it like it is,' he said. 'Next time you go out there it'll be all cleaned up. No blood. No gore.'

She nodded. 'Okay.'

But her wide eyes told him she was still picturing it. 'You're still thinking about it,' he said.

'I'm not,' she denied, chewing on her bottom lip.

Gareth took a step closer to her, wanting to reach for her but clenching his hands at his sides. 'Yes, you are.'

She gnawed on her lip some more and he noticed she'd chewed all her gloss off.

'Look. I'm trying, okay?' she said, placing her palm flat against his chest. 'Just back off for a moment.'

Her hand felt warm against his chest and he waited for her to push against him but her fingers curled into the fabric of his scrub top instead and Gareth felt a jolt much further south. As if she'd put her hand down his scrubs bottoms.

Oh, hell. Just hell.

Now he was thinking very bad things. Very bad ways to calm her down, to take her mind off it.

For crying out loud, she was a freaked-out second-year resident who needed to get back to the lac and get the stupid thing sutured so he could free up a bed. Gareth had dealt with a lot of freaked-out people in his life—the wounded, the addled, the grieving.

He was good with the freaked out.

But not like this. Not the way he was thinking.

Hell.

And that's exactly where he was going—*do not pass 'Go', do not collect any money*—because all he could think about now was her mouth.

Kissing it. Giving her a way to *really* forget what was beyond the door.

It was wildly inappropriate.

They were *at work,* for crying out loud. But her husky 'Gareth?' reflected the confusion and turmoil stirring unrest inside him.

The look changed on her face as her gaze fixed on his mouth. Her fingers in his shirt seemed to pull him nearer and those freckles were so damn irresistible.

'Oh, screw it,' he muttered, caution falling away like confetti around him as he stepped forward, crowding her back against the door, his body aligning with hers, his palms sliding onto her cheeks as he dropped his head.

Billie whimpered as Gareth's lips made contact with hers. She couldn't have stopped it had her life depended on it. Her pulse fluttered madly at the base of her throat and at her temples. Everything was forgotten in those lingering moments as his mouth opened and his tongue brushed along her bottom lip.

Back and forth. Back and forth. Again and again.

Maddening. Hypnotic. Perfect.

The kiss sucking away her breath and her thoughts and her sense. Transporting her to a place where only he and his lips and his heat existed. The press of his thighs against hers was heady, her breasts ached to be touched and her belly twisted hard, tensing in anticipation.

She didn't think she'd *ever* been kissed like this. And she never wanted it to stop.

She slid her hands onto his waist, anchoring them against his hips bones, feeling the broad bony crests in her palms, using them to pull him in closer, revel in the power of his thighs hard against her, fitting their bodies together more intimately.

A groan escaped his mouth, deep and tortured, as if it was torn from his throat and then Gareth pulled away, breathing hard as he placed his forehead against hers, staying close, keeping their intimate connection, not saying anything, just catching his breath as she caught hers.

'You okay now?' he asked after a moment, looking down into her face.

Billie blinked as she struggled to recall what had happened before the kiss. To recall if there had been anything at all—*ever*—in her life before this kiss.

He groaned again, his thumb stroking over her bottom lip, and it sounded as needy and hungry as the desire burning in her belly. 'We can't…do this here,' he muttered. 'We have to get back.'

She nodded. She knew. On some level she knew that. But her head was still spinning from the kiss—it was hard to think about anything else. And if that had been his plan, she couldn't fault it.

But it was hardly a good long-term strategy.

He took a step back, clearing his throat. 'You all right to do the lac now?' he asked.

The laceration. Right. That's what had happened before the kiss. She tried to picture it but her brain was still stuck back in the delicious quagmire of the kiss.

'Give me five minutes and then come to the cubicle. I promise it'll be a different sight altogether.'

Billie nodded. 'Okay.' She shifted off the door so he could open it.

And then he was gone and she was alone in the staff-room, her back against the door, pressing her fingers to her tingling mouth.

* * *

Billie took a few minutes to review the chart of her head lac patient. His blood alcohol was way over the limit. He'd gone through a glass window. The X-ray report was clear—no fractures, no retained glass—but she pulled it up on the computer to satisfy herself nonetheless.

The laceration wasn't deep but it was too large for glue.

Ten minutes later she pulled back the curtains of the cubicle. Gareth faltered for a moment as he looked at her and she didn't have to be a mind-reader to know what he was thinking.

The way his eyes dipped to her mouth said it all.

'All ready,' he said briskly, as he indicated the suture kit laid out and the dramatically changed wound. The blood was gone, leaving an uneven laceration, its edges stark white. It followed the still-sleeping patient's hairline before cutting across his forehead.

Billie swallowed as she took in the extent of it. It wasn't going to be some quick five-stitch job.

'Size six gloves?'

She nodded as she dragged her gaze back to Gareth, thankful for his brisk professionalism.

'Go and scrub,' he said. 'I'll open a pair up.'

Billie stepped outside the curtain and performed a basic scrub at the nearby basin. When she was done she waited for the water to finish dripping off her elbows before entering the cubicle again. She reached for the surgical towel already laid out and dried her hands and arms then slipped into her gloves, hyper-aware of Gareth watching her.

She took a deep breath as she arranged the instruments on her tray to her liking and applied the needle to the syringe filled with local anaesthetic.

She could do this.

She glanced at Gareth as she turned to her sleeping patient. His strategy had worked—she wasn't thinking about the gruesome chore ahead, all she could think about was the kiss.

'Good grief,' she said, screwing up her nose as a blast of alcoholic fumes wafted her way. 'Think I should have put a mask on.'

'Aromatic, isn't he?'

'It's Martin, right?' she enquired of Gareth as if they'd been professional acquaintances for twenty years. As if he hadn't just kissed her and rocked her world.

Gareth nodded. 'Although he prefers M-Dog apparently.'

Billie blinked. 'I'm not going to call him M-Dog.'

Gareth laughed. 'I don't blame you.'

'Martin,' Billie said, raising her voice slightly as she addressed the sleeping patient.

Gareth shook his head. 'You don't have much experience with drunk teenage boys, do you? You need to be louder. You don't hear much in that state.'

She quirked an eyebrow. 'You talking from experience?'

He grimaced. 'Unfortunately, yes.'

Billie returned her attention to the patient. 'Martin!' she called, louder, firmer. But still nothing.

'Allow me,' said Gareth. He gave the teenager's shoulders a brisk hard shake and barked, 'Wake up, M-Dog.'

The teenager started, as did Billie, the demand cutting right through her. It was commanding, brooking no argument.

And *very* sexy.

Had he learned that in the military?

'Hmm? What?' the boy asked, trying to co-ordinate himself to sit up and failing.

Billie bit down on her cheek to stop from laughing. 'I'm Dr Keyes,' she said as Martin glanced at her through bloodshot eyes. 'I'm going to put some stitches in that nasty gash in your head.'

'Is there going to be a scar?' he asked, his eyes already closing again. 'Me mum'll kill me.'

Billie figured that M-Dog should have thought about that before he'd gone out drinking to excess. But, then, her sister Jessica had never been big on responsible drinking either. She guessed that was part and parcel of being a teenager.

For some, anyway.

'Martin, stay with me,' Billie said, her voice at the right pitch and command for M-Dog to force his bleary eyes open once again. 'I'm going to have to put a lot of local anaesthetic in your wound to numb it up. It's going to sting like the blazes.'

He gave her a goofy grin. 'Not feelin' nuthin' at the moment.'

Billie did laugh this time. 'Just as well,' she said, but the teenager was already drifting off. 'Okay,' she muttered, taking a deep breath and picking up the syringe. She glanced at Gareth. 'Here we go.'

Gareth nodded. She looked so much better now. She had pink in her cheeks, her freckles were less obvious and she'd lost that wide-eyed, freaked-out expression.

Billie's hand trembled as she picked up some gauze and started at the proximal end of the wound, poking the fine needle into the jagged edge and slowly injecting. M-dog twitched a bit and screwed up his face and Billie's heart leapt, her hand stilling as she waited for him to jerk and try and sit up. But he did nothing like that, his face settling quickly back into the passive droop of the truly drunk.

Clearly he *was* feeling no pain.

Gareth nodded at her encouragingly and Billie got back to work, methodically injecting lignocaine along the entire length of the wound, with barely a twitch from M-Dog. By the time she'd fully injected down to the distal end, the local had had enough time to start working at the beginning so she got to work.

Her stomach turned at the pull and tug of flesh, at the dull thread of silk through skin, and she peeked at Gareth.

'Talk to me,' she said, as he snipped the thread for her on her first neat suture.

He glanced at her, his gaze dropping to her mouth, and the memory of the kiss returned full throttle. 'What do you want me to talk about?'

Not that, Billie thought, returning her attention to the job at hand. *Anything but that.* The military. The *incident* that had caused his demotion, which Helen had hinted at earlier. But neither of those seemed appropriate either. Not that appropriateness hadn't already been breached tonight. But they needed to steer clear of the personal.

They'd already got *way* too personal.

'Tell me about the patients out there.'

And so he did, his deep steady voice accompanying her needlework as they wove and snipped as a team.

CHAPTER FIVE

THE REST OF the night and the two following were better than Billie could have hoped. The gore was kept to a minimum and she managed to get through them without any more near nervous breakdowns.

Or requiring any more resuscitative kissing.

Not that she wasn't aware of Gareth looking out for her. Which should probably have been annoying but which she couldn't help thinking was really sweet. *And* kind of hot.

She knew the last thing he needed was having a squeamish doctor to juggle as he ran the night shift with military-like efficiency—overseeing the nursing side as well as liaising with the medical side to ensure that the ER ran like a well-oiled machine. But he seemed to take it in his stride as just another consideration to manage.

He was clearly known and well respected by both nurses and doctors alike, he was faultlessly discreet, he knew everybody from the cleaning staff to the ward nurses, he knew where everything was and just about every answer to every procedure and protocol question any of them had.

By the time she'd knocked off on Sunday morning she was well and truly dazzled.

St Luke's was lucky to have Gareth Stapleton.

Which begged the question—why wasn't he *running* the department as he apparently used to? What had happened to cause his demotion? What was *the incident* Helen had made reference to? Annabel Pearce, the NUM, was good too, but from what Billie could see, Gareth ran rings around her.

Billie yawned as she entered the lift, pushing the button for the top floor. Her mind drifted, as it had done a little too often the last couple of days, to the kiss. She shut her tired eyes and revelled in the skip in her pulse and the heaviness in her belly as she relived every sexy nuance.

Not only could Gareth run a busy city emergency department but he could kiss like no other man she knew.

And Billie had been kissed some before.

She'd had two long-term relationships and a few shorter ones, not to mention the odd fling or two, including a rather risqué one with a lecturer, in the eight years since she'd first lost her virginity at university. She liked sex, had never felt unsatisfied by any of her partners and wasn't afraid to ask for what she wanted.

Essentially she'd been with men who knew what they were doing. Who certainly knew how to kiss.

But Gareth Stapleton had just cleared the slate.

She wet her lips in some kind of subconscious memory and grimaced at their dryness. Between winter and the hospital air-con they felt perpetually dry. She pulled her lip gloss out of her bag and applied a layer, feeling the immediate relief.

The lift dinged and she pushed wearily off the wall and headed to the fire exit for the last two flights of steps to the rooftop car park. She jumped as a figure loomed in her peripheral vision from the stairs below, her pulse leaping crazily for a second before she realised it was Gareth.

And then her pulse took off for an entirely different reason. 'You took the stairs?' she said in disbelief. '*All* eight floors?'

Of course he had. Super-nurse, freaked-out-doctor whisperer, kisser extraordinaire. What wasn't the man capable of?

'Of course.' He grinned. 'It's about the only exercise I get these days.'

Billie shook her head as they continued up the last two flights, which was torture enough for her tired body. By the time they'd reached the top and Gareth was opening the door, her thighs were grumbling at her and she was breathing a little harder.

Of course, that could just have been Gareth's presence.

Was it her overactive imagination or had his 'After you' been low and husky and a little too close to her ear?

She stepped out onto the roof, her brain a quagmire of confusion, thankful for the bracing winter air cooling her overheated imagination. She zipped up her hoody and hunched into it.

Gareth was hyper-aware of Billie's arms brushing against his as they walked across the car park to their vehicles. 'You on days off now?' he asked.

She nodded. 'Three. How about you?'

'Me too.' Which meant they'd be back on together on Wednesday. An itch shot up Gareth's spine.

Fabulous.

Three days didn't seem long enough to cleanse himself of the memory of the kiss and he really needed to do that because Billie, he'd discovered, was fast becoming the only thing he thought about.

And that wasn't conducive to his work. Or his life.

The last woman he remembered having such an instantaneous attraction to wasn't around any more, and it had taken a long time to get over that. In fact, he wasn't entirely sure he'd managed it yet. He grimaced just thinking about the black hole of the last five years.

Billie was in the ER for six months and the next few years of her life would be hectic, with a virtual roller-coaster of rotations and exams and killer shifts sucking up every spare moment of her time. She didn't have time to devote to a relationship, let alone one with a forty-year-old widower.

They were in different places in their life journeys.

They reached their cars, parked three spaces from each other, and he almost breathed a loud sigh of relief.

'Well...' he said, staring out at the Brisbane city skyline, 'I guess I'll be seeing you on Wednesday.'

She looked like she was about to say something but thought better of it, nodding instead, as she jingled her keys in her hand. 'Sure,' she murmured. 'Sleep well.'

Gareth nodded, knowing there was not a chance in hell of that happening. 'Bye.'

And he turned to walk to his vehicle, sucking in the bracing air and refusing to look back lest he suggest something *crazy* like her coming to his place and sleeping off her night shift there.

In his bed.

Naked.

Get in the car, man. *Get in the car and drive away.*

He opened the door, buckled up and started the engine. It took a while for his car to warm up and the windscreen to de-mist and he sat there trying not to think about Billie, or her sparkly dress, or her cute freckles.

Or that damned *ill-advised* kiss.

A minute later he was set to go and he reversed quickly, eager to make his escape. Except when he passed her car, it was still there and she was out of it, standing at the front with the bonnet open, looking at the engine.

He groaned out loud. No, no, no! *So close.* He sighed, reversing again and manoeuvring his car back into his car space. He disembarked with trepidation, knowing he shouldn't but knowing he couldn't not offer to help her.

'Problem?' he asked, as he strode towards her.

Billie looked at him with eyes that felt like they'd been marinating in formaldehyde all night. If possible he looked even better than before. 'It won't start,' she grumbled.

'Is it just cold?'

'No. I think the battery's flat.'

'Want me to give it a try?'

'Knock yourself out,' she invited.

Gareth slid into the plush leather passenger seat and turned the key. A faint couple of drunken whirrs could be heard and that was it. He placed his head on the steering-wheel. Yep. Dead as a doornail.

'Did you leave your lights on?' he asked, as he climbed out.

She shook her head. She'd taken her hair out of her pony-tail and it swished around her face, the tips brushing against the velour lettering decorating the front of her hoody. Her nose was pink from the cold.

'The car automatically turns them off anyway.'

Of course it did. It wasn't some twenty-year-old dinosaur. A pity, because if it had been he could have offered her a jump start. But with the newer vehicles being almost totally computerised, he knew that wasn't advisable.

'Do you have roadside assistance?'

'No. I know, I know...' Billie said, as he frowned at her. She rubbed her hands together, pleased for the warmth of her jeans and fleecy top in her unexpected foray into the cold. 'It expired a few months back and I keep meaning to renew it but...'

His whiskers looked even shaggier after three nights and his disapproving blue eyes seemed to leap out at her across the distance. 'You're a woman driving *alone* places, you should have roadside assistance.'

Billie supposed she should be affronted by his assumption that she was some helpless woman but, as with everything else, she found his concern for her well-being completely irresistible.

He sighed. 'I'll drive down to the nearest battery place and get you one,' he said.

Billie blinked as his irresistibility cranked up another notch. Was he crazy? 'It's *Sunday*, Gareth. Nothing's going to be open till at least ten and I don't know about you but

I'm too tired to wait that long.' She shut her bonnet. 'I'll get a taxi home and deal with the battery this afternoon after I've had a sleep.'

Gareth knew he was caught then. He couldn't let her get a taxi home. Not when he could easily drop her. Unless she lived way out of his way. 'I'll give you a lift,' he said. 'Where do you live?'

He hoped it was somewhere *really* far away.

Billie would have been deaf not to hear the reluctance in his voice. And she was too tired to decipher what it meant. Tired enough to be pissed off. 'You don't have to do that, Gareth,' she said testily, fishing around in her bag for her mobile phone. 'I'm perfectly capable of ringing and paying for a taxi. I could even walk.'

She watched a muscle clench in his jaw. 'Don't be stupid,' he dismissed. 'You've worked all night and I'm here with a perfectly functioning car. It makes sense. Now... Where. Do. You. Live?'

She glared at him. 'Only a really *stupid* man would call a tired woman stupid.'

Gareth shut his eyes and raked a hand through his hair, muttering, 'Bloody hell.' He glanced at her then. 'I apologise, okay? Just tell me where you live already.'

'Paddo.'

Paddington. *Of course she did.* Trendy, yuppie suburb as befitted her sparkly dress and expensive car. 'Perfect. You're on my way home.' He was house-sitting in the outer suburbs but she lived in his general direction.

She folded her arms. He could tell she was deciding between being churlish and grateful. 'If you're sure you don't mind?'

Gareth shook his head. 'Of course not,' he said, indicating that she should make her way to his car. 'As long as you don't mind slumming it?'

Billie shot him a disparaging look. 'I'm sure I'll manage.'

Gareth nodded as she passed in front of him. The question was, would he?

CHAPTER SIX

THEY DROVE IN silence for a while as Gareth navigated out of the hospital grounds and onto the quiet Sunday morning roads. He noticed she tucked her hands between her denim-clad thighs as he pulled up at the first red traffic light.

'Are you cold?' he asked, cranking the heat up a little more.

'Not too bad,' she murmured.

Gareth supposed the seats in her car were heated and this was probably a real step down for her. And maybe when he'd been younger, before life had dealt him a tonne of stuff to deal with, he might have felt the divide between them acutely.

But he'd since lived a life that had confirmed that possessions meant very little—from the pockmarked earth of the war-torn Middle East to the beige walls of an oncology unit—he'd learned very quickly that *stuff* didn't matter.

And frankly he was too tired and too tempted by her to care for her comfort.

Her scent filled the car. He suddenly realised that she'd been wearing the same perfume last Saturday night but he had been too focused on the accident to realise. Something sweet. Maybe fruity? Banana? With a hint of vanilla and something…sharper.

Great—she smelled like a banana daiquiri.

And now it was in his car. And probably destined to be so for days, taunting him with the memory.

She shifted and in his peripheral vision he could see two narrow stretches of denim hugging her thighs, her hands still jammed between them.

'So,' Gareth said out of complete desperation, trying to *not* think about her thighs and how good they might feel wrapped around him, 'you called yourself Dr Keyes...the other night. With M-Dog.'

Yep. Complete desperation. Why else would he even be remotely stupid enough to bring up *that* night when they were trapped in a tiny, warm cab together, only a small gap and a gearstick separating them, the kiss lying large between them?

But Billie didn't seem to notice the tension as she shrugged and looked out the window. 'It's easier sometimes to just shorten it. Ashworth-Keyes is a bit of a mouthful at times and, frankly, it can also sound a bit prissy. I tend to use it more strategically.'

'So drunk teenagers who go by the name of M-Dog don't warrant the star treatment?'

Billie turned and frowned at him, surprisingly stung by his subtle criticism. 'No,' she said waspishly. 'Some people respond better to a double-barrelled name. There are some patients, I've found, who are innately...snobbish, I guess. They like the idea of a doctor with a posh name. Guys called M-Dog tend to see it as a challenge to their working-class roots...or something,' she dismissed with a flick of her hand. 'And frankly...' she sought his gaze as they pulled up at another red light and waited till he looked at her '...I was a little too...confounded by our kiss to speak in long words. I'm surprised I managed to remember my name at all.'

Billie held his gaze. If he was going to call her on something, he'd better get it right or be prepared to be called on it himself. She might be helplessly squeamish, she might not be able to stand up to her family and be caught up in the sticky web of their expectations but she'd been taught how to hold her own by experts.

There was nothing more cutting than a put-down from a surgeon who thought the sun shone out of his behind.

'Yes,' he said after a moment or two, his throat bobbing as he broke eye contact and put the car into gear. 'That was… confounding.'

Billie almost laughed at the understatement. But at least he wasn't denying it. They'd studiously avoided any mention of the kiss since it had happened, but it *was* there between them and she knew he felt it as acutely as she did.

She'd spent the last couple of days telling herself that it hadn't meant anything. That it didn't *count*. That Gareth had used it only as a strategy to snap her out of her situation.

But it had still felt very real.

They accomplished the rest of the trip in silence, apart from her brief directions, and Gareth pulled up outside her place in under ten minutes.

'Thank you,' she said, unbuckling.

Gareth nodded. 'No problems,' he murmured, as he let the car idle.

He waited for her to reach for the door handle but she didn't. 'No. I mean for everything,' she said. 'For just now but also for the other night. For what you did. For how you helped…calm the situation. For the kiss.'

Gareth swallowed hard as Billie once again mentioned the one thing he was trying hard not to think about. She'd been right when she'd said it was confounding and he wished she'd just leave it alone so he could put it away in his mental too-hard-to-deal-with basket.

'Don't,' he said. 'Don't thank me for that.' Confounding or not, it hadn't been proper. 'What happened…it pretty much constitutes sexual harassment.'

Her snort was loud in the confined space between them, the world outside the warm bubble of the car forgotten.

'That's rubbish, Gareth,' she said. 'Kissing me at work is only sexual harassment if I didn't want or encourage it, if it was unwelcome, and while I appreciate you trying to give me a pass on my behaviour, you can be damned sure I wanted you to kiss me, very *very* much. We're not *just* two people who met at work, we're not *just* colleagues, and you know it. We're both adults here so let's not pretend there hasn't been a thing between us since the accident.'

Gareth looked at Billie, her brown eyes glowing at him fiercely, her chest rising and falling, stretching the fabric of her hoody in very interesting ways across her chest. He found it hard to reconcile this woman with the one who had been a pale wreck over a head lac or vomiting at the scene of an accident.

He nodded. 'Of course. You're right. I apologise.'

The *thing* pulsed between them and God knew he wanted her now.

He looked away, inspecting her house through the windscreen for a few moments, the heater pumping warm air into the already heated atmosphere. It was one of those old-fashioned worker cottages that had been bought for a song twenty years ago, renovated and sold for a goodly sum.

'Do you want to come in? For a coffee.'

Gareth shut his eyes against the temptation, feeling older and more tired than he had in a long time. 'Billie,' he murmured, a warning in his voice.

Billie looked at his profile. 'Don't trust yourself, Gareth?' she taunted.

He looked at her, her lip gloss smeared enticingly, a small smile playing on her mouth, a knowing look in her eyes, and his tiredness suddenly evaporated.

He didn't trust himself remotely.

'Billie... This isn't going to happen.'

She looked at him for long moments. 'Why not?'

The enquiry could have come across sounding petulant. If she'd pouted. If she'd injected any kind of whine into her voice. But she didn't. She just looked at him with that slight smile on her mouth and asked the very sensible, very reasonable question.

They wanted each other. They were both single and of age. *Why not indeed?*

Gareth sighed. 'You're, what, Billie? Twenty-seven?'

She shook her head. 'Twenty-six.'

Gareth groaned. Dear God, It was worse than he'd thought. 'I'm forty years old,' he said. 'I think you need to play with boys your own age.'

'You think I'm too young for you?'

He nodded. 'Yes.' *Way* too young. 'And...'

'And?' She skewered him with her gaze. 'You think I'm too forthright, don't you?'

'No! I don't care about that. I like forthright women.' His wife, a complete stranger at the time *and* stone-cold sober, had come right up to him in a bar and kissed the life out of him in front of everyone.

'Well, then?'

'Billie...' he sighed. 'I'm at a different stage of my life than you are. You've got many years ahead of you, with a lot of hard work and dedication to get where you're going. You don't have the time to devote to serious relationships and I'm—'

'It's *coffee*, Gareth,' she interrupted.

Gareth shook his head at her, his gaze drifting to her mouth, the gloss beckoning, then back to her earnest brown eyes. 'It's not just coffee and you know it.'

She shrugged then slid her hand onto his leg. 'Would that be such a bad thing?'

A hot jolt streaked up Gareth's thigh and he was instantly hard. His hand quickly clamped down on hers as it moved closer to ground zero. 'Give me a break here, Billie. I'm trying to do the right thing.'

'How very *noble* of you,' she murmured glancing at her hand held firmly in place by his before returning her attention to him. 'Look...I understand that you think I need kid gloves after the other night but I really don't need you looking out for me in *this* department. I think this *is* the right thing.'

Gareth's sense of self-preservation told him otherwise. There wasn't one part of him that believed their *coffee* session would be the end of it. And, despite her confidence right now, he'd met enough doctors in this stage of their careers to know how many relationships didn't make it.

His wife's death had left Gareth very wary. It had taken a huge chunk out of him. One that had never grown back. He had no intention of lining up for another pound of flesh. And something told him Billie could do exactly that.

So she wanted a fling? Not going to happen. Not when they worked together.

'I'm not into recreational sex.'

'Really?'

She smiled then, her voice clearly disbelieving. She tried to move her hand further north but he held tight for a few moments before finally giving away to her insistence. Gareth watched her palm move closer to his crotch, torn between stopping her again and grabbing her hand and putting it where his groin screamed for attention.

She halted just short of his happy zone and he tore his gaze away from her neat fingernails so very, very close to his zipper.

'I think you must be the only man in the world who doesn't see the value in a little harmless physical release,' she said.

Gareth absently noticed that the windscreen was fogging up on the inside and tuned in to the roughness of her voice and the heaviness of his own breathing as the pads of her fingers brushed awfully close to nirvana. He knew if he didn't stop this now, he wouldn't.

And with his normal self-control lulled due to lack of sleep, he was just weary enough to succumb.

'*I think* you're tired,' he said, turning his face to look at her. 'We're both tired. *I think* people can make bad decisions when they're tired.'

She slid her hand home and Gareth shut his eyes, biting

back a groan as pleasure undulated through the fibres deep inside his belly and thighs.

'I'm awake now,' she murmured, her voice husky in the charged atmosphere. 'And I gotta say…' she paused to give his erection a squeeze '…you don't feel that tired to me.'

God.

She was trying to kill him.

Gareth gave a half-laugh. 'Trust me,' he said, his eyes opening as he gathered his last scrap of self-control and re-moved her hand from his hard-on, '*that* is a really unreliable measure of tiredness. Of anything, for that matter.'

Billie's stomach plummeted, and not in a good way, as she placed her hand back between her thighs. She'd felt so sure that she'd be able to persuade Gareth to stay and she squirmed a little in the seat to ease the ache that had started to build between her legs in delicious anticipation.

'I'm sorry, Billie.'

She tossed her head and looked out the window. 'It's fine,' she said.

Billie supposed she should feel embarrassed or mortified. And perhaps if she'd been more mentally alert she might have been. Hell, if she'd been more mentally alert she probably wouldn't have propositioned him at all.

Or been so damned persistent.

No doubt the mortification was yet to come but for now she just felt disappointed.

'I just…don't want you to do something that you might regret tomorrow,' he continued. 'This kind of step needs to be taken when all your faculties are intact and I don't want to be on your dumb-things-I-did list, Billie. We have to work together for the next six months and I've been around long enough to see how awkward that can be in the workplace.'

Billie nodded. Just her luck to develop a thing for the first man she'd ever met who didn't think with his penis.

She turned to look at him. 'You have one of those?'

He frowned and his eyes crinkled and he looked all sexy

and sleepy and perplexed and she wanted to drag him into her house, into her bed *so freaking bad* even if it was just to snuggle and sleep. 'One of what?' he asked.

'A dumb-things-I-did list.'

His frowned cleared and then he laughed. 'Oh, hell, yeah.'

His laughter was deep and rich and warm, a perfect serenade in their intimate cocoon, so nearly tangible Billie felt as if she could pick it up and wrap it around her like a cloak. Interesting lines buried amidst all that stubble bracketed his mouth and she squeezed her thighs together tight, trapping her hands there.

Hands that wanted to touch him.

Billie didn't have that kind of list, although she suddenly wished she did. Even if it meant he was at the top. Although no doubt there were plenty who would think living out her sister's dreams to keep her parents happy was a really dumb thing to do.

The unhappy thought pierced the intimacy and Billie stirred. She didn't want it in here with them. She unbuckled her seat belt. 'Thanks for the lift.'

Billie reached for the handle and pulled; the door opened a crack and cold air seeped in as she half turned her body, preparing to exit. But Gareth's hand reached across the interior, wrapping gently around her upper arm.

'You understand it's not about *not* wanting you, right?'

Billie's heart almost stopped in her chest. She looked over her shoulder at him. He looked bleak and tired and *torn*.

'I know,' she murmured, and then, without thinking about it, she leaned across the short distance between them and kissed him quick and hard.

For a brief few seconds she felt him yield. Whiskers spiked her mouth and scraped her chin and she tasted the spice of his groan.

And then she pulled away—pulled away before she did something crazy like straddle him—and exited the car without looking back.

CHAPTER SEVEN

WORKING WITH GARETH on Wednesday wasn't as excruciating as Billie had thought it was going to be. She *had* suffered a degree of remorse over her behaviour and *had* been prone to episodes of acute embarrassment during her days off whenever she remembered how persistent she'd been, but he'd soon put her at ease with his brisk professionalism.

It helped that he didn't come on until the afternoon so she was already in the groove when she first fronted him. And then, of course, he was focused and businesslike as always and by teatime she'd almost forgotten that she'd groped him in his car and more or less invited him into her bed but been knocked back.

She didn't regret it, as he had predicted. She doubted she would have regretted it if he'd taken her up on her offer either.

But she was mindful of how it must look to him. How *she* must look. What he thought of her she had no idea. She'd known him for less than two weeks and in that time she'd swung wildly from being a vomiting, hyperventilating wreck to a penis-squeezing vamp.

That made her cringe.

He seemed so sophisticated, so *together,* compared to her.

Why it should be a concern she didn't want to think about. He was right—she had a tough few years ahead of her career-wise and being in a relationship had not been part of her plans.

Her parents and all the extended members of the Ash-worth-Keyes surgical dynasty had said the same thing. Specialising was hard on your social life and not a lot of relationships survived. Career first, personal life later.

So, yeah, Gareth's words of wisdom had resonated with her the other morning.

But still... He made her want things. And specialising wasn't one of them.

Gareth's mobile rang as he sat at the table in the staffroom. He was pleased for the reprieve. Billie was sitting opposite him and he swore she was just wearing that lip gloss now to drive him crazy. Thankfully Kate and Lindy, two of the junior nurses on the afternoon shift, were having their break as well and the three women were engaged in a conversation about television vampires.

Amber's picture flashed on the screen and he smiled as he slid the bar across to answer. 'Hey, sweetheart,' he said as he answered the phone. Billie glanced at him, a little frown drawing her brows together, and he got up and wandered over to the sink, his back to the table. 'Everything okay?'

Apparently not. His stepdaughter was crying so hard he could barely make out her garbled reply. A hot spike of concern lanced him. 'Amber?' he said, trying to keep his voice down and devoid of alarm. 'What's wrong?' he demanded.

He was pretty sure she was telling him she was outside. 'You're here?' he asked, already turning and heading for the door, aware on a subliminal level of Billie's interest but too worried about Amber for it to register properly.

'I'm coming now,' he said, as he hung up and pulled the door open.

Thirty seconds later he was stalking out into the main thoroughfare, spotting Amber looking red-faced and dishevelled near the triage desk, the long fringe of her pixie cut plastered

to her forehead in a way that she usually wouldn't be seen
dead wearing.

His heart leapt into his mouth. 'Amber?' He strode towards her.

When she flung herself against his chest and dissolved
into even more tears, Gareth knew it had to be bad. His and
Amber's relationship had been fairly tempestuous since her
mother had died and public displays of affection had been
strictly forbidden.

He didn't blame her. Amber had been fifteen when Catherine had been diagnosed and had died five months later
from breast cancer. Being angry at him was easier than being
angry at the entire world. Although she'd been there too.

Patients in the waiting area and members of staff looked
on curiously as Amber's loud honking cries continued and
didn't seem likely to abate any time soon. He led her into the
nearby nurses' handover room, which was essentially a cubicle with three sides of glass. But it had a door he could shut,
was relatively soundproof and with various posters stuck
on the walls they were obscured somewhat from full view.

'What happened?' he asked, as he shut the door after
them. 'Did you break up with Blaine?'

Amber's cries cut off as she glared at him. 'Only three
months ago.'

He held up his hands in apology. 'Really?'

'Yes,' she snapped.

Amber had been a good kid but also, in many ways, a
typical teenager—everything an overblown drama—and
then she'd been a *grieving* teenager, which had put her into
a whole different category. It had been like watching a train
wreck and trying to be there to pick up the pieces, when she'd
let him. Things had been particularly fraught.

And now she was a pissed-off young woman.

And he *still* couldn't tell when her tears were serious or
just the I-broke-my-fingernail-and-it's-all-your-fault variety.

Catherine had always known.

Gareth realised suddenly he hadn't thought about Catherine in a while and, with Amber looking at him with those big green eyes the exact shade of her mother's, guilt punched him hard in the chest.

'Okay, so…what *is* the matter?'

Amber sniffled and dragged a ball of crumbled-up paper out of her bag and handed it to him. Gareth took it, hoping it wasn't some 'Dear John' letter that he really *did not* want to read. He unravelled it, the wrinkled page quickly revealing itself to be a lab report.

A sudden spike of fear sliced into his side. He looked at this kind of report every day in his job. But he and Amber had a history with these reports too—not one he ever wanted to repeat.

He ironed it out with his hands as he scanned it.

The top left-hand corner had Amber's personal details. Name. Address, Date of birth. Allergy status. The next line leapt out at him.

BRCA1—positive.

Gareth's breath caught in his throat. His heart thumped so hard his ribs hurt. His vision tunnelled, narrowed down to the stark brevity of that line.

She had tested positive for a faulty gene that dramatically increased her risk of developing breast cancer. The disease that had killed her mother.

Crap!

'I didn't think you wanted the test,' he said, looking at a red-eyed Amber as his brain scrambled to absorb the shocking news.

She shrugged in that belligerent way he was used to but it somehow lost its effectiveness when she looked so devastated. 'I changed my mind.'

Gareth sat down on the nearest chair. 'I thought we were going to talk about it together before you decided.'

'I…couldn't,' she said. 'And anyway it was…spur of the moment.'

Gareth looked down at the page again. 'I didn't want you to go through this by yourself, Amber.'

'I didn't…I had counselling. The cancer centre wouldn't let me do it without.'

He shook his head at the things she must have been going through these last few weeks. He rang or texted most days but Amber was busy at uni, living the college life. Occasionally she rang or texted back. Sometimes happy, sometimes not. Sometimes because she needed money or a place to crash for the night.

And he got that. But this…he would have thought she'd want him around for this.

'I could have been there for you.'

Gareth had had to stop himself five years ago from demanding she take the test there and then. Catherine's death had been devastating and the thought that Amber might have inherited the gene had been too much to bear. He hadn't been able to reach in and rip the cancer out of Catherine, but he could protect Amber from her mother's fate.

They could be forewarned. Forearmed.

But the oncologists and Amber's psychologist had counselled against it at such a young age. And he'd *known* they were right. Logically, he'd known that. She hadn't needed that extra burden at that point, not when she had probably been years away from making any concrete decisions over a potentially positive result.

But his fear hadn't been logical.

Amber may not have been his daughter by blood but he'd been with Catherine since Amber had been a cute five-year-old with two missing front teeth and he loved her as fiercely as if she were his own.

She shook her head. 'I didn't want to…worry you.'

He gave her his best don't-kid-me look. 'You think I don't worry about you, Amber?'

Her eyes filled with tears then, so like her mother's, and

his heart broke for the grief Amber had endured in such a short life.

'What am I going to do, Gareth? I have a forty to eighty per cent chance of developing breast cancer. Do I get a double mastectomy? Do I line up to have my uterus removed and never be able to have a baby?' She looked at him with those big green eyes swimming in tears. 'What man's going to want me with no boobs, Gareth?'

She started to cry again and Gareth stood, reaching for her and sweeping her into his arms. 'Shh,' he said, hugging her close just like when she'd been a kid and fallen off her bike, skinning her knee and denting her pride.

Back in the days when there hadn't been five years of angst and grief and blame between them.

'Hey,' he said, as he stroked her hair, letting her cry, raising his voice above the wrenching noise of it. 'Firstly, you and I are going back to the clinic together so we can have a nice long talk about options.'

He made a mental note to make the first available appointment. 'Secondly, these aren't decisions you're going to need to make for a long time, sweetheart. This just means we have to be more vigilant. And I'm going to be there for you every step of the way, okay?'

'Okay,' she said, and cried harder.

'Thirdly...' This was the hardest one. He didn't relish having to talk to Amber about sexuality and desire. She'd generally thought any topics like that were private and female and not up for discussion with her stepfather.

But if she'd been a patient asking these questions, searching for answers, he wouldn't have hesitated to reassure her.

Gareth prised her gently off his chest and looked down into her red swollen eyes. 'Do you think your mother losing a breast made me love her any less? Made her any less desirable to me as a woman?'

He half expected her to rebel. To screw up her face and say, 'Eww, gross, Gareth,' which had been pretty much her catchphrase from thirteen onwards. But she didn't, she just shook her head at him. 'But you already had a relationship with Mum. You had to love her regardless of her…boob situation.'

Gareth smiled at Amber's typical reluctance to use correct anatomical words. 'I loved your mother from the first moment I met her. And it had nothing to do with her *boobs*.'

'It's still not the same,' Amber dismissed.

Gareth squeezed her arms. 'Any man who can't see past your physical self to the amazing woman you are inside isn't worth your time, Amber. Life's short, sweetie, you don't need me to tell you that. Too short to waste on men who aren't worthy.'

Amber smiled up at him through her tears. She slid her hand onto his cheek and patted his stubble like she used to when she was little and had been endlessly fascinated by its scratchiness. She'd never known her father and Gareth's stubble had been intriguing. She dropped her hand.

'I don't think they make men like you any more.'

Gareth smiled down at Amber, feeling closer to her than he had in a long time. 'Yes, they do, sweetie,' he said. 'And I still have my service revolver for the others.'

She smiled again then pulled away, turning her back to him as she looked absently through the patches of glass to the hustle and bustle of the department.

'Do you think I'm vain for worrying about my boobs?' she asked eventually. 'About someone wanting me when so many women are dead? When Mum is dead?'

Gareth slid his hand onto her shoulder and gave it a squeeze. 'Of course not, Amba-San.' Her old nickname slipped out. She normally chided him for using it these days but not today. 'You can't think about something like this and not think about how it affects you in every way. But you are getting ahead of yourself sweetheart. Way ahead.'

Amber turned and nodded and Gareth's hand slipped

away. 'I'm sorry. I guess the results freaked me out a little. They tried to talk to me at the clinic about them but I just ran.'

'It's okay, we'll go back there together in the next couple of days, okay?'

Amber nodded. 'Just promise me you'll find me the best plastic surgeon in the country to give me new boobs if or when this whole thing becomes a reality.'

Gareth smiled, encouraged by her *if*. 'I promise I'll find you the best breast man I can.'

Amber screwed up her nose and said, 'Eww, gross, Gareth,' but she was smiling and she walked easily into his arms, accepting his hug.

When they pulled apart he slipped his hands either side of her face and cradled it like he used to. 'How about you come over tonight? I don't get off till nine but we can get takeaway and watch one of those dreadful chick flicks you like so much.'

Amber laughed. 'Oh, the sacrifice.' She rubbed her cheek into his big palm for long moments before pulling away. 'It's okay. Carly knows. I'm going out with her tonight and drinking way too much tequila.'

Gareth nodded. The father in him wanted to caution her against drinking to excess but he'd been twenty himself once. And Carly was a very sensible young woman. If she knew the circumstances then Gareth had absolute faith she wouldn't let Amber get too messy. Those two had had each other's backs since they'd been nine.

'Okay,' he said. 'Are you sure you're going to be all right?'

Amber nodded. 'Talking with you helped.'

He smiled. 'You can always talk to me, Amba-San.'

'I know. Sorry I can be such an ingrate sometimes. It just still…gets me sometimes and I just don't know what to do with it. It makes me so…angry, you know?'

'Yeah,' Gareth said. He knew *exactly* how she felt. 'I know.'

There was a brief knock on the door and it opened.

'Gareth,' the triage nurse said, peeking her head around the door, 'assault victim, multiple injuries, blunt chest trauma, in a bad way. Ten minutes out.'

He looked at Amber. 'Sorry.'

She smiled and gave him a quick hug. 'It's fine. I'm already late and Carly will be waiting for me.'

'I'll call you tomorrow,' he said.

'Okay.'

'I love you, Amber,' he said.

She gave his stubble a pat again. 'Love you too,' she said, as she departed the room.

Gareth's gaze followed her, his heart beating a steady determined tattoo. Cancer couldn't take her too.

Billie almost collided with Amber as she hurried out of the handover room. 'Sorry,' Billie called after the young woman, who continued on but not before Billie had noticed the tear-streaked face.

Billie glanced up to find a grim-looking Gareth standing in the open doorway, tracking the woman's progress. Clearly something had transpired between them. Was it another nurse she hadn't met yet? Or another colleague? Or a patient's relative?

Whatever it was, it was obviously intense.

Her stomach twisted hard.

CHAPTER EIGHT

'YOU READY FOR THIS?'

Billie looked up from staring down at her gloves, the ambulance siren loud as it screeched to a halt metres from them. It echoed around the concrete and steel bay, reverberating against her chest, drumming through her veins.

She stiffened at Gareth's propriety. 'Yes.'

He still looked all kinds of grim. Was that him mentally preparing for what they were about to see or was it to do with the mysterious woman? A hot knot of emotion lodged in her chest and Billie realised she felt jealous. Which was utterly insane. She had no claim over him to justify jealousy. And it was hardly an appropriate time to feel the hot claw in her gut.

An assault victim was fighting for his life in the back of an ambulance, for crying out loud.

But it was there. It just *was*.

And his *concern* for her rankled. It was courteous and kind and thoughtful. And she hated it.

She didn't need his pity, his propriety or his patience.

Well…she didn't *want* them anyway. She didn't want him looking at her as some cot case to coddle and hand-hold and treat with kid gloves.

She didn't want him to look at her as a chore.

Not when she saw him in an entirely different light.

A paramedic opened the back door of the ambulance. 'It's going to be messy,' Gareth warned.

Billie's irritation ramped up another notch despite the strong stir of nausea in her gut. 'I know,' she snapped.

Did he really think she *didn't* know?

And then it was action stations as the paramedics hauled the gurney out of the back and pushed it quickly towards them, the intensive care paramedic reeling off a handover as they all accompanied the briskly moving trolley.

'Corey Wilson, twenty-two-year-old male, found in an alley in the city with multiple injuries, presumed assault. Unresponsive, bradycardic, hypotensive. Pupils unequal but reactive to light. Intubated on the scene, a litre of Hartmann's given, wide-bore IV access both arms.'

They entered the resus bay and Billie's hands shook as she helped get the beaten and bloodied young man across to the hospital trolley. An endotracheal tube protruded from his mouth and a hard collar protected his neck during the process.

Within a trice the ambulance gurney was gone and Billie was staring into Corey's grotesquely bruised face. Dried blood was smeared everywhere, his eyes swollen and ringed in black and purple. Her stomach turned over.

His shirt, split up the middle by a pair of paramedic shears, hung down his side, revealing more blood and bruising on his chest as ECG dots were slapped in place.

Denise Haig, the emergency consultant, who hadn't yet gone home for the day, barked orders at everyone. 'Let's get him assessed and to CT,' she said.

The oxygen saturations on the monitor were decreased and Denise looked at Billie and said, 'Listen to his chest.'

Billie fought against the urge to turn away, fought the pounding in her own chest, concentrated on her breathing, staring at Corey's chest rather than his face as she shoved her stethoscope in her ears and listened. She felt Gareth's eyes on her but refused to look at him as she quickly assessed both lung fields.

She was part of this team and she would work with them

to save Corey, no matter how affected she was by his battered body.

'Chest sounds decreased on the right, almost absent,' Billie reported. 'Lot of crepitus.'

Which was hardly surprising. Corey looked like he'd taken a real beating to the chest, broken ribs were a given. The oxygen saturations fell further and Corey's heart rate, which had been worryingly slow, suddenly shot up.

'Check his JVP,' Denise said.

Billie was on autopilot now, the adrenaline in her system keeping her going, elevating her to a higher place, allowing her to do her work yet stay removed from the horror of it.

The hard collar obscured his neck veins from her view and she had to peer through the side window to assess it. His jugular bulged ominously. 'Pressure elevated,' Billie said. She flicked her gaze to his windpipe, which appeared, from what she could see, to be skewed to one side. 'Trachea's deviated.'

Denise nodded. 'Tension pneumo. Put in a chest tube, stat,' she ordered.

Billie's hands shook as someone thrust a pair of sterile gloves at her. No time for a proper surgical scrub. This was *emergency* medicine with a capital E. The build-up of air in Corey's chest from a fractured rib puncturing his lung was affecting his venous return and he needed urgent chest decompression.

She looked up as she shoved her right hand into the right glove. *Gareth.* He nodded and smiled at her. 'Good to go?'

Concern radiated from his eyes and Billie was determined to dispel it immediately. She nodded back. 'You got the pack?'

He dragged a small mobile trolley over with all she would need already laid out. He reached over and squirted some liquid antibiotic on Corey's chest and briskly cleaned a section of skin mid-axilla with some gauze. When it was reasonably clear of dried blood he doused the area again with the brown antiseptic agent.

'Your turn,' he said.

Billie moved closer, reaching for the scalpel. In a normal clinical setting she'd be gowned and masked, she'd inject local, the patient would be draped. But Corey didn't have that time, this was down and dirty. This was life and death.

She was conscious of the screaming of alarms around her and the battering of her pulse through her head as she quickly located the right spot. This wasn't her first chest tube, although it was her first tension pneumo.

Billie made a small incision. Blood welled from the cut and she forced her shaking knees to lock.

'Forceps,' she said, concentrating hard on keeping her voice steady as she handed the scalpel back to Gareth.

He passed her the forceps and she bluntly dissected down to the pleura, puncturing it with the tip of the forceps. She inserted her finger into the hole and swept away a soft clot she could feel there, her stomach revolting at the action.

'Tube,' she said, not looking at Gareth, not looking at anything other than her finger in someone's chest and concentrating on not throwing up. He handed it to her and she placed the tip into the hole, using the forceps to feed it in, advancing it until all the drainage holes lining the tip were inside the chest cavity.

The whole procedure was accomplished in less than a minute and her hands shook as she stripped the gloves off.

The oxygen sats improved almost immediately and Corey's heart rate decreased.

'Well done,' Gareth murmured, just loud enough amidst the chaos for only the two of them to hear. He handed her a pair of regular gloves and connected a drain bottle to the end of the tube.

Their celebration of her competency was short-lived, however, as suddenly a torrent of blood flowed out the tube, draining quickly into the collection device. Before Billie's eyes it filled to halfway and she swallowed back a retch as more rushed in, forming a thick red sludge.

'Haemo-pneumo,' Gareth said.

Denise nodded. 'Not surprising. Push two units of O-neg.'

'Pupils are blown.'

'Right,' Denise said to Gareth. 'Get on to Cat Scan. Tell them we're coming around. Where the hell is Neuro?' she asked no one in particular.

They were snapping the side rails in place when the monitor alarmed again. The heart rate, which had started to slow down again after the chest tube insertion, suddenly flicked into a dangerous tachy-arrythmia. Denise felt through the side windows in the collar. 'We've lost his pulse.'

The rails came down again as Denise issued another rapid-fire set of orders, rattling off some drug doses.

Billie couldn't stop looking at the drainage from the chest, the bottle was three-quarters full now. She couldn't block out the screaming of the alarms. Corey's life was literally draining away.

Just like Jessica's had that night.

He was twenty two and dying. It was too cruel. She wanted to throw up, faint *and* burst into tears.

'Billie!'

Denise's shrill command broke through her inertia. Billie looked at her. 'I said start chest compressions.'

Billie nodded. She faltered as she placed her gloved hands on Corey's chest, looking down at the dried blood streaking his ribs and belly. 'I'll do it,' Gareth said, stepping forward.

'No!' Gareth's interference suddenly snapped Billie out of it. She didn't care how much she wanted to stop and throw up right now. She needed to prove she could do this. To Denise. *To Gareth*. To her long-dead sister.

And most especially to herself.

She had to know she could get past her physical reaction to the gore and rawness of emergency medicine. She had to know that she could pigeonhole the human tragedy that threatened to overwhelm and cripple her and do what needed to be done.

* * *

They worked on Corey for forty-five minutes. Billie sought and found her earlier state of removal as she pounded on his chest. Going through the motions, following directions but all the time placing her mental side, her emotional self, elsewhere. Buried somewhere at the back of her brain.

Not thinking about Corey or his age or what his last moments must have been like or that he was dying surrounded by strangers. Not thinking about the drainage bottle being changed. Or the repeated unsuccessful zaps to the chest. Removing herself from the arrival of his mates and the shouting and loud angry sobs as they were told he was critical and they had to wait.

Just doing her job.

Her arms ached. Her muscles screamed at her. Gareth offered to take over but she declined. Several others offered as well but she refused.

And even when Denise called time of death and everyone stopped and stepped away, it took a moment or two for Billie to realise, continuing the compressions until Gareth touched her arm and said, 'You can stop now, Billie.'

She'd been so focused on the action, on breathing with each one, on the way her gloved fingers looked against Corey's sternum, she'd zoned out everyone else.

Billie looked around at the defeated faces, the downcast eyes and stepped back herself.

Denise stripped off her gloves. 'Thanks, everyone,' she said.

Half an hour later Denise approached Gareth. 'I need you in on the chat with the relatives,' she said.

Gareth nodded. They'd been waiting for Corey's parents to arrive. His mates were still in the waiting room, subdued now as they waited for news about their friend, but as it was against hospital policy to provide information to people who weren't relatives, they hadn't yet been told of Corey's passing.

'You going to do it now?' he asked.

'No.' She shook her head. 'Billie's going to do it. But I'll be there. And so will you.'

Gareth glanced over at Billie, who was writing up Corey's notes. He'd sat in on one too many of these not to know how harrowing they were—he wouldn't wish them on his worst enemy. He certainly wouldn't wish it on a woman he'd come perilously close to bedding a handful of days ago.

'Come on, Denise,' he murmured, 'do you really think she's up to it? Don't you think she's been through enough trauma today?'

Demise nodded briskly. 'I know. But if she wants to do this job, then talking to relatives is all part and parcel of it. Better to get the first one over and done with.'

He quirked an eyebrow at her. He'd worked with Denise for five years. She was good. Fair. Shrewd. And a little old school. 'Tough love?'

'Got to sort the wheat from the chaff.'

'You don't have to do it tonight. She should have knocked off thirty minutes ago.'

Denise shrugged. 'Billie's a good doctor but she's not cut out for this. I know it and I suspect you know it too. It's better that she figures that out early than waste years of her life specialising in a field that doesn't suit her talents because she watched too many ER dramas on TV.'

Gareth shot her a look full of recrimination. 'Steady on.'

'Oh, come on, Gareth, don't tell me you haven't seen them year after year, lining up to work here because it's been glamorised on television.'

Sure, he had, but those residents rarely lasted the distance. 'I think her reasons are a little deeper than that.'

'Okay. Maybe you're right. Maybe it's because she felt a calling or because Mummy and Daddy hot-shot surgeons want her to do it. Whatever the reason is behind her wanting to screw up her life, it's still a bad idea.'

Gareth had to admit that Denise made very valid points

but he believed there were some things that people just had to work out for themselves. And that Billie's reasons for setting her sights on emergency medicine *were* a lot more complicated than watching too much television medical drama.

'I think she'll figure it out,' he said.

'This should help.'

'She's due off,' he reiterated.

'She can do this then go home,' Denise said briskly, her mind clearly made up. 'You coming or do you want me to grab one of the other nurses who were in there?'

Gareth sighed. No way could he abandon Billie to Denise's tough love. He put down his pen. 'I'm coming.'

CHAPTER NINE

BILLIE LOOKED DOWN at the notes. Her hands were still trembling and there was a persistent numbness inside but writing the notes helped.

And when she got home—which *could not* be soon enough—there was a bottle of wine in the fridge that would also help.

But for now it was pen on paper.

And she took comfort in that. Writing notes she *could* do. She could be clinical and detached in notes. She could look back at the situation and couch it in neat medical terms. The words formed a mental barrier between the chronology of the event and the *emotion* of the event. They allowed her to report the frantic last moments of Corey Wilson's life in a simple, detached way that she only hoped stayed with her when she got home tonight.

'Billie.'

Billie looked up from the chart as Denise approached, with Gareth hovering behind. They looked very serious and a prickle shot up her spine as she wondered what kind of hell they had in store for her now.

'Corey's parents are here. I know your shift finished half an hour ago but as you were involved in the resus I thought it would be good experience for you to talk to them.'

Billie stilled. Watching Corey Wilson die had been hard enough. Now she had to deliver the dreadful news to his parents too? She'd rather stick herself in the eye with a poker than have to tell these people their twenty-two-year-old son was dead.

She glanced at Gareth, whose face was carefully neutral.

'His parents are going to want to talk to people who were there at the end,' Denise said. 'And it's vital that we provide that for them. That we put aside our emotions and feelings and do whatever we can to make it a little bit easier for them.'

Denise stopped for a moment, as if she was allowing some time for that message to sink in.

'One of the most important things you'll ever do as a doctor is tell someone that their loved one has died,' Denise said. 'It's never easy, especially in sudden death, and it doesn't get any easier, no matter what anyone tells you. But it is a skill you need to learn. I'll be there,' she said. 'So will Gareth.'

Billie nodded. She knew Denise was right. That whatever she was feeling was nothing compared to what those two strangers waiting in that room off the triage desk with the mismatched furniture and the bland prints on the wall were feeling.

'Okay,' she murmured huskily, and rose on legs that felt like cement.

Billie sat on her couch two hours later, her hand still trembling as she sipped on her third glass of wine. She'd been home for an hour, and apart from turning on the fire and collecting the wine bottle and a glass she hadn't moved from this position.

Feelings of helplessness hit her in waves and she blinked back tears, rocking slightly as she fanned her face, breathing in and out through pursed lips as if she were running an ante-natal class. And then the words that she'd written in Corey's chart would come back to her and she would calm down again, holding onto every sentence like she had when she'd been in with his parents, repeating what she'd memorised from the notes to cut herself off from the emotion, to stop herself from breaking down in front of them.

But then the echo of Chantelle Wilson's wounded howl would break through the cool clinical words and the waves would buffet her again. It had been chilling. And the way she'd crumpled, folded in on herself...Billie had seen her mother do that when her sister had died and hated that she was the one inflicting the wound on another mother.

Billie had seen a few deaths in her first year but they'd been elderly people or terminal patients. Not like this.

Not this total waste of a human life that had barely begun.

She'd never looked into the eyes of a mother and had to use the D word. Denise had cautioned about using euphemisms for death as they'd walked to the room. People were in a highly emotional state, they needed clarity, she said.

But even so it had dropped like a stone into the atmosphere of that room and then the howl had sucked all the oxygen away.

A loud knock at the door interrupted her pity party and she flinched, dragging her gaze away from the fire. 'Billie, it's Gareth.' Another knock. 'Open up.'

Tears formed in her eyes again and she concentrated on whistling air in and out of her lips. She was barely hanging on here. If she saw him, if he was kind, she'd break down for sure.

'Billie!' Another sharp rap on the door. 'I know you're in there. I swear I'm going to kick this door in if you don't open it.'

Billie believed him. Unfortunately, Mrs Gianna next door was probably already calling the police due to Gareth's insistent knocking.

The last thing she needed was a police car pulling up in her driveway.

She took another fortifying sip of her wine before rising on legs that felt like wet string, desperately reaching for the cool detachment of her notes. She scrubbed a hand over her face to dispel the dampness on her cheeks as she walked to the door.

Billie drew in a steadying breath as she placed her hand on the knob. *You can do this.*

'Hi,' she said, as she opened the door, the cold night air like a perfect balm on her simmering emotions.

Gareth had expected to find a tear-stained wreck. But Billie looked exactly the same as when she'd left the hospital. Same jeans and shirt clinging in all the right places, a little on the pale side, her freckles standing out but a look of stoic resolve embedded on her features.

'Hi,' he said. 'I called by to check on you.'

She nodded. 'I'm fine.'

Except the tiny crack in her husky voice and the way she had to quell the tremble of her bottom lip with her teeth told him differently.

Gareth's heart went out to her. Incidents like this took their emotional toll on everyone involved. They left a little chink in a person's soul. And those chinks could build up if they were ignored.

'Billie...' he said softly. 'His head injuries were too massive. He probably coned. Nobody could have saved his life.'

'I know that,' she said testily.

He inclined his head. 'I know you do.'

He watched as Billie's throat bobbed. 'Don't be nice to me,' she warned. 'I can't deal with that.'

'Okay...' Gareth buried his hands in the pockets of his leather jacket. 'What are you doing?'

'Getting drunk.'

He smiled. 'Very Australian of you.' He earned a ghost of a smile back. 'You know, you could have joined us at Oscar's. A bunch of us went there at the end of the shift.'

Oscar's was the bar across the street from St Luke's. A very profitable business, especially after shifts like these.

She shrugged. 'I didn't feel like company.'

Gareth understood the sentiment but he'd learned through

his years in the military that drinking alone after the kind of day she'd had was not good.

What she needed was camaraderie. To be with people who understood the horror of what she'd been through.

'It helps to talk it out with people who know, you know?'

Billie nodded. 'Yeah. But I *really* didn't feel like company.'

And Ashworth-Keyes' did not break down in front of people.

Gareth regarded her for long moments—it looked like *he* was going to be her sounding board tonight. He knew he could sure as hell do with some alcoholic fortification. Between Amber's news and the bloodied trauma of Corey's death, a beer would really hit the spot right now.

And, besides, there was no way he could leave her to drown her sorrows solo.

'Do you have beer?' he asked.

'Yes.'

'Can I join you?'

'If you want.' She shrugged.

Billie turned on her heel and left him to follow her. She was already feeling stronger for the distraction of something else, someone else to think about.

'Take a seat,' she threw over her shoulder, as she passed the lounge room and headed for the kitchen. The house was dark, she hadn't bothered with lights, but she knew the low glow from the fire provided enough radiance for Gareth to see where he was going.

She opened the fridge door and plucked a beer from the back. She didn't know what type it was. Some boutique beer her father favoured and had left in her fridge for the odd time he dropped around. Usually to check how she was going with her studies and whether she was being a good little Ashworth-Keyes. Telling her how proud they were of her, how proud *Jessica* would be of her.

Billie entered the lounge room, noting Gareth had succumbed to the toastiness of the room and slipped out of his jacket. He was wearing a long-sleeved knit shirt like she was, except his had a round neck as opposed to her V. It obscured the fascinating hollow at the base of his throat, the one she'd used to ground herself during her harrowing talk with the Wilsons whenever emotion had threatened to overwhelm her.

She also noticed he'd chosen to sit on the three-seater where she'd been sitting, and not on one of the single chairs.

Billie handed him the beer as she plonked down next to him, leaving a discreet *just two colleagues talking* distance between them. She picked up her glass of wine and turned slightly side on to him. He followed suit so they were facing each other.

She raised her glass towards him. 'To traumatic shifts.'

Gareth smiled. 'To *getting through* traumatic shifts,' he said, tapping his beer bottle against the side of her glass.

They both drank, their gazes turning to the fake flames of the gas fire bathing the room in a cosy glow. For long moments silence filled the space between them.

Billie looked down into the deep red of her Merlot, the flame reflected in the surface. 'I can't do it,' she announced quietly.

Gareth turned his head. 'You were fine, Billie. And you were great with the Wilsons.'

At another time his praise might have filled her with pride but it was little consolation right now. She looked at him. 'Denise knows I can't do it.'

He shrugged. 'So prove her wrong.'

Billie shook her head. 'She thrives on it. *You* thrive on it.'

'And you don't?'

She shook her head. 'It turns my stomach.'

Gareth watched the reflection of the flames glow in her eyes as he asked her the same question he'd asked her before. 'So…why *are* you doing it, Billie?'

Blind Freddie could see that her heart wasn't in it.

'Oh…now,' she said, taking a sip of her wine. 'That's…'

'Long and complicated?' he said, repeating her answer from the last time he'd asked.

She gave a half-smile. 'Yes.'

Gareth held his beer up to the light. The fluid level had barely moved from the top after his two mouthfuls. 'I'm not going anywhere for a while.'

Billie looked into the fire. Where did she even start? She'd spent so much of her life pretending this was what she wanted that it was hard to remember sometimes why it wasn't.

'My sister died when she was sixteen. In a car accident. She was quite the rebel, always in trouble for something. She sneaked out of her window one night and went joy riding with some friends and never came back again.'

Gareth shut his eyes at the news. What an awful time that must have been for Billie. For her family. 'I'm sorry,' he murmured.

'Thank you.'

'What was her name?'

'Jess,' Billie said. 'Jessica.'

'Were you close?'

Billie nodded. 'She was two years older than me but, yeah…we were close. Close enough to confide in me that not only didn't she want to carry on the mighty Ashworth-Keyes tradition of being a surgeon, she didn't want to be a doctor at all. She wanted to be a kindy teacher.'

'And she couldn't tell your parents that?'

Billie snorted. 'Ashworth-Keyes' are *not* kindergarten teachers.'

'Even if it makes them happy?'

She shook her head. 'What on earth has happiness got to do with it? Ashworth-Keyes' are *surgeons*. My parents, my uncles, an assortment of cousins, my grandfather, my great-grandfather. From the cradle our glorious future in a gleaming operating theatre is talked about and planned incessantly. Everything revolves around that. There is no other career path in my family.'

'Oh, I see,' Gareth said, even though he really didn't.

As a father all he cared about was Amber being happy and well adjusted and contributing to society. But he *was* beginning to understand the conditioning that Billie had been subjected to.

'Of course, my father thought he would have sons, like all of his brothers had, to carry on the family tradition, but unfortunately he was saddled with girls. Still, to give him his due, he took it on the chin and settled into indoctrinating us too. He wasn't going to be *the* Ashworth-Keyes to break with tradition just because he had *girls* who might want to do something unpredictable and girly.'

'It sounds like there was a lot of pressure on you.'

Billie nodded. 'Jessica didn't know how to tell them. And she didn't want to be a disappointment to them. So she just kept telling them what they wanted to hear. That she was going to do medicine. That she was going to become a cardiothoracic surgeon just like them.'

'And would she have eventually, do you think, had she lived?'

Billie shrugged. 'I don't know. She was certainly bright enough. Straight As, even with no studying. Not like me, who had to work for my As. But she was very strong-headed. I doubt she would have done anything she didn't want to do. She was just keeping them sweet, I guess, putting off the inevitable confrontation.'

'Sounds like she was trying to tell them something with her rebellion.'

Billie nodded. 'Yes. I think all her reckless behaviour was really just a cry for help. I think it was her way of trying to goad them into disowning her and then she'd be free to do what she wanted.'

'But it didn't work out so well?'

Billie thought about that awful night. The police. Waking to crying at midnight. Her crumpled mother, a lot like Mrs Wilson. Her disbelieving father. 'No. It didn't.'

Gareth waited for a few moments. Took a mouthful of his beer. 'And so you decided to step into her shoes,' he said eventually. 'To be the daughter they thought she was going to be.'

Billie looked at him sharply. 'Yes.'

He nodded. 'Did you even want to be a doctor at all?'

'Of course,' she said derisively. 'I'm an Ashworth-Keyes, aren't I?'

'Billie.'

The reproach in his voice pulled her up. 'Yes,' she said. 'I did. I've always wanted to be one.'

'But not a cardiothoracic surgeon, right?'

Billie shook her head. 'Not a surgeon at all, I'm afraid. Or an ER consultant. I wanted to be a GP.'

CHAPTER TEN

GARETH LOOKED AT HER, surprised. A general practitioner? The complete opposite of an emergency physician. But he knew, instantly, it was the right fit for her.

Billie was an *excellent* doctor. He'd watched her with patients. She liked to take her time with them, which they loved but wasn't always conducive to the ER. And it wasn't laziness, it was thoroughness.

And her bedside manner was one of the best he'd ever witnessed.

She enjoyed the little stuff that the others had no patience for, the attention to detail, and she loved a medical mystery, loved getting to the bottom of what was making a person sick.

He knew without a shadow of doubt that she'd make a brilliant GP. And, God knew, there weren't enough of them.

'What's wrong with being a GP? They're just as vital to the health care system.'

Billie snorted. Her father would have apoplexy at hearing such sacrilege. 'Ashworth-Keyes' aren't—'

'GPs,' Gareth finished off with a grimace. 'And you never told them either?'

She shook her head. 'I was relying on Jessica being the trail blazer. Rocking the boat first, upsetting the apple cart, and then I could sneak in behind, wanting to be a GP. I figured they'd be so grateful I still wanted to be in the medical profession at all that they'd give me a pass. But then my mother…she completely fell apart after Jessica died. She didn't operate for an entire year.'

Billie paused and rubbed her arms, feeling suddenly cold again. 'She was just this…shell, this…husk. She'd just sit for hours and stare at the wall. Apart from looking at my sister's dead body, it was the most frightening thing I've ever seen.'

Gareth slid his hand onto hers. He thought back to how emotionally whammied he'd been when Catherine had died. It had only been his duty to Amber, her emotional distress and neediness that had kept him from spiralling into his own pit of despair. Amber had looked at him sometimes with fear in her eyes, fear that he just might sink into depression and then what would she do?

So he didn't. But there had been days when it had been very hit and miss.

'I'm sure it was,' he murmured.

'Finally, she came out of it. Finally, she came back to her old self, started seeing patients, resumed her surgical schedule, but she never seemed quite as robust again, like she could still break at any second. And somewhere along the way she decided that *I* was going to take Jessica's place. That *I* was going to live the life that Jessica had supposedly wanted because that would be the perfect way to honour my sister. She became obsessed with it and there were so many times when she seemed so fragile I just couldn't tell her the truth so I…went along with it. I couldn't bear the thought of her…going back to that dark place… Pretty pathetic, huh?'

Gareth shook his head. He understood the weight of parental expectations and the things people did to live up to them, and that was without a tonne of grief behind it all.

His father had never quite forgiven him for eschewing a job as his building apprentice to become a nurse. *Real men weren't nurses,* according to him. It was only joining the military that had made it more respectable in his eyes.

And, he guessed, GPs weren't real doctors to Billie's high-flying parents. 'I think we all do things we don't want to in order to keep from disappointing the people we love,' he said.

Billie nodded. It sounded like Gareth had some experience in that department too. 'What did you do?' she asked.

Gareth withdrew his hand and looked away from her as he took a long drag on his beer. When he was done he rolled it back and forth in his hands, watching the firelight catch the gold in the label.

'I became NUM of the ER,' he said eventually.

Billie blinked. He hadn't *wanted* to be NUM? Now, *that* she hadn't been expecting. She'd have thought that would be the pinnacle of his civilian career.

'For who?' she asked his downcast head, as his inspection of the shiny label continued.

Gareth glanced up at Billie. The firelight gilded the warm brown of her eyes and added pink to her cheeks. 'My wife.'

Billie stilled. His *wife?* He was *married?* But…she'd been in the tearoom when a couple of the junior nurses had been swooning over him and had gleaned there that he wasn't married. *And* he didn't wear a ring. Neither did he have a white mark where one had recently been taken off.

So then he must be divorced.

He had to be. Gareth had been nothing but honourable. She couldn't believe that he would have kissed her—no matter what psychological state she'd been in—if he hadn't been free and clear to do so.

She felt ill just thinking about it.

And the way she'd come on to him. His frankness about the…*thing* between them. He wouldn't have allowed that, acknowledged their vibe, if he'd been married.

He wouldn't be here now, surely?

Billie swallowed hard, battling against the invective raring to leap from her throat, and simply asked, 'Why?'

He frowned. 'Why did I do it for her?'

Billie nodded, still fighting the urge to demand he clarify his marital status immediately.

Gareth steeled himself to answer. He didn't talk about Catherine often, especially to colleagues or people he barely knew. But he did know Billie. Probably better than a lot of people he'd worked with for years.

And he knew her even better after the events of today, after their talk tonight.

Besides…there was just something about a fire that encouraged confidences.

'Because she was dying,' he said, capturing Billie's gaze. 'And she was happy and proud and excited for me and because she knew it would be more regular working hours for Amber after she was gone.'

'Amber?'

'Our daughter.'

It all clicked into place then for Billie. He was a widower. He had a daughter. Suddenly she knew Amber was the young woman she'd seen him with at teatime. 'She was there today…Amber…'

'Yes.'

Relief flooded through her. Cool and soothing. 'I'm sorry…about your wife. How long ago?'

'Five years.

'What cancer was it?'

'Breast,' Gareth said. 'From diagnosis to her death was five months.'

Billie shook her head sadly. Cancer was a real bitch. 'How old was she?'

'Catherine,' Gareth said. He wanted Billie to know her name. 'Her name was Catherine and she was forty. We'd been married for ten years.'

'How did Amber take it?'

He shrugged. 'She was fifteen. She blamed me.'

Fifteen. About the same age Billie had been when Jessica had died. Not the same thing as losing your mother but still an utterly devastating experience.

'Why did she blame you?'

'I was on tour in the Middle East when Catherine found the lump. She waited until I came home almost two months later before she did anything about it.'

Billie couldn't contain the gasp that escaped her throat at that particular piece of information. 'Why did she wait that long?'

Gareth felt the old resentment stir. 'For a lot of reasons—none of them very sound. She didn't want to worry me or Amber. She didn't want to cause a fuss and have me brought home over something she was sure was nothing. She didn't really think it was anything because she'd always had lumpy breasts. She didn't want to go through the investigations alone...'

Billie watched as he ticked each one off on a finger. The firelight caressed the spare planes of his face, picking up the grooves on either side of his mouth, the whiskers shadowy there. She almost reached out and traced the fascinating brackets.

'The list goes on,' Gareth continued, and he sounded so grim and bleak Billie had the strangest urge to put her arms around him. 'Not that it would apparently have mattered that much, the cancer was so aggressive. But, in her bad moments, Amber felt betrayed by Catherine. She felt that her mother had put me and my job—*"the stinking army"*, I believe were her exact words—first. That Catherine had loved me more than her own flesh and blood.'

Billie winced. 'That must have been rough.'

He shrugged. 'She was a grieving teenager. She was lashing out. I was just the dad. The stepdad at that.'

'She's not your biological child?'

He took a sip of his beer, shaking his head. 'No. She was five when Catherine and I met. Cute as a button. Both of them were.'

He grinned suddenly, raising the bottle once more, his lips pressed to the rim, still smiling. And it was so sexy, so masculine her stomach took a little dive. He obviously had wonderful memories.

'You loved her.'

He nodded as he looked directly at her. 'Of course. She filled up my heart.'

Billie was touched by his sincerity. Not some stupid fake Valentine's Day sentiment but something deep and honest.

She'd never known love like that.

'I'm sorry,' she said again, topping up her wine and taking a sip, watching him over the rim of her glass.

He shrugged and looked back at his beer but not before she glimpsed a dark shadow eclipsing the blue of his eyes. It spoke of pain and grief and *stuff* that hid in dark recesses, hijacking a person when they least expected it.

How long had the grief consumed him? And was that what had caused the incident that Helen had spoken about on her first day, the one that had seen him demoted?

She knew it was none of her business but sipping on her wine, feeling warm and floaty, she knew she was sufficiently lubed to ask. 'So why aren't you still NUM? I understand there was some kind of…incident that resulted in your demotion?'

Gareth looked up at her sharply. An *incident?* 'Where'd you hear that?'

She shrugged. 'The grapevine.'

Gareth was speechless for a moment then he laughed. It was good to know that some things at St Luke's never changed. Clearly it didn't matter if there was no ammunition for gossip—people would just make it up.

He drained his beer. 'There was no *incident*,' he said, as he placed his empty bottle on the table. 'Amber became independent. She graduated from high school, went off to college, got a car and a part-time job. I stepped down because I didn't need to work regular hours any more.'

Billie frowned. 'You just…stepped down?'

'Yep.'

'But…why? Surely managing an emergency department in a tertiary hospital is a prestigious career opportunity? How do you just walk away from that?'

Gareth could hear the incredulity in her voice. He guessed for someone who had grown up where prestige mattered above everything else, it was a big deal.

'It's easy when you don't care about prestige.'

Billie blinked. She'd had prestige rammed down her throat from a very early age. No matter how many times she'd fantasised about telling her parents where they could stick their aspirations for her, she'd never for a moment imagined that she'd walk away from them. And Jessica's death had made that near on impossible anyway.

She wished she had even an ounce of Gareth's resolve.

'But you must be highly qualified?'

'Sure. I spent a decade in field hospitals, triaging the wounded fresh from battle. I did multiple tours in the Middle East.'

'And you really didn't want to be NUM with all *that* experience?'

He shook his head. 'Nope, I *really* didn't. Being in charge of a civilian unit is not like being in the military. There's too much paperwork and being stuck in an office or going to round after round of meetings.'

Billie nodded. Gareth had obviously been very hands-on during his overseas tours. He exuded vitality and energy and she could just imagine him in head-to-toe khaki under the blades of a chopper with an injured soldier lying on a gurney as the sand whipped up around him.

He certainly strode around St Luke's like a man very comfortable in his environment. Like there was nothing that could be thrown at him that he hadn't already seen.

Somehow she couldn't quite picture him sitting in a white-walled office at some dreary quality or bed-management meeting.

'I guess St Luke's must be a little tame for you.'

'Nah. I've had more than enough excitement to last a lifetime.'

'But you thrive on it.' She'd said it earlier and it seemed even more so now. 'Why didn't you join up again?'

'I have to be here. For Amber.'

Especially now. Amber needed him to be here more than ever at the moment.

'It was okay being away for long periods of time while Catherine was still alive but I'm *it* now. I'm her only family. I can't abandon her even if she is independent and doesn't need me like she did when she was fifteen. And besides…' he rubbed his fingers along his jaw '…trauma medicine, field medicine…it's tough. Mentally tough. I have enough images in my head to fuel nightmares for the rest of my days. I don't see the point in adding to them.'

Goosebumps broke out on Billie's arms at the rasp of scraped whiskers. Her nipples followed suit. He was looking at her with shadows in his eyes again. Her heart almost stopped in her chest as she thought about the things he must have seen. The danger he'd been in.

'Were you scared?'

Gareth shook his head at Billie's husky question. 'I was never near the action. I was safe.'

She quirked an eyebrow. 'Are you ever truly safe in a war zone?'

He gave her a half-smile. 'We were safe.'

The smile played on his mouth and her gaze dropped to inspect it. Orange glow from the flames licked across his lips and she had the sudden urge to try them out. See if they were cool like the beer or scorching hot like the fire.

Billie had her money on the latter and suddenly felt pretty hot herself. 'Do you want another beer?' she asked, as the silence grew between them.

Gareth roused himself. Two beers around this woman would not be a wise move. He'd been dreaming about her in his bed for days now. The last thing he needed was anything that loosened his inhibitions and ruined his common sense. 'No. I should get going.'

Billie quelled the urge to protest the notion out loud.

She didn't want him to go. And she didn't think he wanted to go either.

He hadn't come in and sat opposite her and spent the whole time lecturing her about getting too involved in her job while drinking tea. He'd sat next to her, drunk a beer, listened to her talk.

And he'd been right. It was better to be around people who understood how you were feeling after a particularly harrowing day at work. People who had been right there, side by side with you.

They were debriefing. Being human.

But she wanted more. And maybe, for tonight—after everything she'd been through today—that was possible?

His palm was flat against his leg and Billie tentatively slid her hand onto his. 'Don't go.'

CHAPTER ELEVEN

GARETH LOOKED DOWN at Billie's hand. It was pale compared to his. There were no rings. No nail polish. No fuss. Just like the rest of her.

His heart thrummed in his chest. Not just at her touch but at what she was offering. He swallowed hard. His interest was already making itself felt inside his underwear.

There were only so many denials in him.

He looked up at her, his speech ready to go on his lips, the words he'd said to her the other morning in the car about being in different places easy to repeat. But she didn't give him the chance. She'd edged closer, pushed her hand higher.

'Gareth,' she murmured.

And any words he'd been about to say died on his lips as she pressed her mouth to his.

He sucked in a breath at her boldness and his senses filled with her. Not banana daiquiri this time. Something much more seductive. Red wine and lip gloss. Every nerve ending in his belly snapped taut as her mouth opened, her tongue touched his bottom lip. She pressed herself closer, her thigh aligning with his, her shoulder brushing his.

'Kiss me,' she whispered, her lips leaving his, travelling along the line of his jaw, nuzzling his earlobe, pulling it into her mouth. A hot flush of goosebumps prickled at his skin and he shut his eyes to their seduction.

'Kiss me,' she repeated, her breath hot in his ear, her

voice a sexy whimper, full and wanton. 'I know I shouldn't want you,' she groaned, her lips heading back to his mouth. 'But I can't stop.'

Her mouth claimed his again and there was nothing light and teasing about it. She opened her mouth and dragged him in, sucking him into the kiss and dumping him in the middle of a thousand carnal delights.

The slim thread of his resistance snapped so loudly Gareth swore it could be heard ricocheting off the walls. He groaned, stabbed his fingers into her hair and yanked her head closer.

'Damn it, Billie.'

And then *he* had the con.

The kiss was his to master and he did, taking control, steering the course, opening his mouth wide and demanding she do the same. Seeking her tongue and finding it, duelling with it. He grabbed her then, sliding his hands around her waist, pulling her towards him, putting his hand on a knee, parting her legs, urging her to straddle him, which she did with complete abandon, rubbing herself against him as their hips aligned perfectly.

Her hands glided to his cheeks as he settled her onto him and from her vantage point above him she returned his kiss. Twisting her head to meet his demands, moaning when his tongue thrust inside her. Would this be how she sounded when his tongue thrust inside her at a point significantly lower than her mouth?

Would she moan? Would she whimper? Would she gasp?

Would she squirm against him like she was now, trying to ramp up the friction between them by rubbing herself back and forth along the length of his erection?

He didn't know. But he wanted to find out.

'Shirt,' she gasped, against his mouth.

Shirt.

A one-word cold shower.

Gareth dug his fingertips into her hips as she reached for the hem of his shirt, battling the demons that told him this was a bad idea, praying they wouldn't win, hoping they would.

He held fast, trapping her between his body and the barrier of his arms. She squirmed in protest, trying to move, to strip him of his shirt. His pants. His sanity.

But he knew if he didn't stop this now, he wouldn't stop at all. Once her hands were on his bare, naked flesh, once his were on hers, he was going to be a goner for sure.

'Billie,' he panted, 'stop.'

Billie shook her head. 'No, no.' She kissed his neck, her hot tongue running up the length of it. 'Please...no.'

Gareth shut his eyes, trying not to think about how good her tongue would feel running up the length of something else.

Her hands reached for his pecs and he covered them with his own, capturing them against his chest and refusing to let them move, to cause any kind of rub or friction.

His libido just wasn't that strong at the moment.

'Billie...' he murmured in her ear, as she collapsed against him in frustration, 'we can't do this.'

Billie couldn't believe what she was hearing. They were so close to getting naked and doing the wild thing. And he wanted it as much as she did, she knew he did.

Why couldn't they do this? Why was he being so damn honourable?

'Why not?' she asked. 'I know you want to.'

Gareth shut his eyes and asked the universe for patience to be forthcoming—ASAP.

'Of course I want to, Billie,' he said, keeping his voice low, turning his head so his lips brushed her hair. He sat with her there for long moments. He needed her to know that this wasn't about what he wanted.

He shifted then, applying pressure to her hips, urging her to sit back a little. Somehow along the way her ponytail had loosened from its clasp, her hair falling forward to form a curtain around her face, and he pushed it back so he could see her.

'But you've been drinking,' he said, peering into her face. With her back to the fire it was heavily shadowed. Her eyes were dark, taupe puddles and he couldn't tell what she was thinking. 'So have I. This isn't the kind of decision we should be making now.'

Billie snorted. 'I've had three glasses of wine, Gareth. I'm hardly messy drunk.'

'And as you well know, consent can't be given under the influence of drugs or alcohol.'

She crossed her arms. 'You want me to sign a waiver?'

'Billie…'

Gareth shut his eyes briefly as she moved, swinging her leg off him and sitting back on the couch, taking care to leave a good distance between them. What seemed like an acre of orange glow flickered between them. He raked a hand through his hair.

She was furious.

'I'm sorry. I just don't want you to regret this tomorrow.'

Billie laughed. She couldn't help herself. She was beginning to wonder about his prowess between the sheets. 'Are you that bad, Gareth?' She almost laughed again at the affronted look he shot her.

'I've never had any complaints,' he said stiffly, and Billie had to admire his restraint. Any other man would have bragged. Any other man might have been tempted to make her retract her deliberately bold statement by resuming what they'd started. But she was fast coming to realise that Gareth Stapleton was not like any other man.

Billie rose from the couch and stalked to the fire. She couldn't sit a moment longer. Not next to him anyway. He was driving her mad and she needed to pace.

She stared into the fake orange flames for a few moments, trying to come up with the right words that would give him some insight into her feelings.

'I think I'm the best judge of what I will and won't regret,' she said eventually.

Gareth stared at the dip at the small of her back and the way it arched up so elegantly to the span of her ribs. He admired the straight line of her shoulders.

'You think I like this?' he murmured. 'You think I think that self-denial is some bloody balm for the soul? Because I don't. But not only are you under the influence, you've also been through some heavy emotional stuff tonight. Using sex as some kind of emotional eraser *isn't* the right way to handle it.'

Billie turned to face him, her arms folded. 'Well, *gee whiz*, Gareth, thanks for the lecture, but how about you let me handle my stuff my way and you handle yours your way, okay?'

'I have had some experience with this, you know.'

He looked kind of grim again and Billie wondered what experience he meant. His time in the military? The horror of the things he must have seen there? Or the things he'd seen during five years in a busy city emergency department?

Or was he thinking about his wife?

Had he used sex after his wife's death to *handle* it?

Had he had a bevy of women, mistresses, who had helped him through it or had his transactions been more…random? Had he preferred hook-ups to any further potential emotional entanglements?

'Okay. So what is the right way to handle it?'

Gareth stood. 'Believe it or not, talking about it with someone who knows.' He shoved his hands in his pockets as he moved closer lest he do something really dumb like think *Screw it* and drag her into his arms. 'Which is exactly what we were doing before we went and…'

'Complicated it?' she supplied.

'Okay…sure.' Gareth had been going to say 'ruined it'. Complicated was far less severe.

'Fine,' Billie said. 'But you should know I'm about all talked out now. I'm going to sit here and finish the bottle of wine. You can either stay and watch me or you can leave. But I must warn you if you stay I *will* be outrageously provocative. I'll probably get grabby. I may even take off my clothes. Because…' she pulled her shirt away from her tummy and fanned it back and forth a couple of times '…it's getting kind of hot in here, you know?'

Gareth nodded. He was burning up.

'So…' She gave him a half-smile. 'Probably best you leave now, unharassed and unmolested.'

Gareth smiled back, glad that she was trying to make light of the situation. 'I think plan B sounds like the wisest choice.'

She raised a derisive eyebrow. 'Imagine my surprise.'

He laughed. 'I'll be off now, then.'

Gareth was relieved, as he followed her to the door, that their earlier antipathy seemed to have dissolved and they were back on a more even footing.

'Thanks for coming over,' she said, as she opened the door and stood aside for him to exit.

It was his turn to lift a derisive eyebrow. 'Really?'

Billie laughed. 'Yes. Really. It did help, doing that talking stuff you're so big on.'

'Really?' He grinned.

Billie rolled her eyes. 'Really. Just don't come over again unless you plan on doing an Elvis.'

'An Elvis?'

She grinned. 'A little less conversation, a little more action.'

Gareth chuckled. Billie Ashworth-Keyes was an intriguing woman. She was a strange mix of smart and unsure, vulnerable and strong, funny and sober. He knew, standing on her threshold tonight, a warm orange glow behind her gilding her chestnut hair, soft yellow from the streetlight caressing her face, that sooner or later he and Billie were going to end up in bed.

Just not tonight.

Sure, he'd been telling himself since they'd met that it

wasn't going to happen but denial seemed useless now. He could feel the power of their attraction in the stir of his loins and the thrum of his pulse. And he knew, even though it was wisest, he wasn't going to be able to ignore the dictates of his body for ever.

He was, after all, only a man. And he wanted her.

He just needed to remember that they couldn't have anything permanent. That underneath her cool, funny façade Billie was a mess. A ticking time bomb ready to explode, and he'd had enough of bombs—metaphorical and actual— to last a lifetime.

She had a lot of things to work out in her life or she was going to wind up completely miserable, and most of it, unfortunately, she was going to have to figure out by herself.

And he didn't want to be collateral damage while she did.

He stared at her mouth for long moments—it really was utterly kissable—before he dragged his gaze back up to hers.

'When we do finally do it, Billie, and I promise you *we will*, I will Elvis your brains out.'

And while she was standing there, blinking up at him, her mouth forming a delicious little O, he smiled and said, 'Goodnight.'

CHAPTER TWELVE

TWO DAYS LATER Gareth sat in a counsellor's office at the cancer clinic with Amber. They were listening to the pros and cons of double mastectomy versus regular intensive screening and hyper-vigilance.

'In short, Amber, we don't recommend such a radical step at such a young age,' Margie, the counsellor, said regarding the mastectomy. 'Certainly not without extensive counselling and taking some time to really think through the implications.'

Margie was a breast cancer survivor herself. She looked to be in her sixties, her hair grey, short and spiky, and Gareth could tell that Amber valued her opinion. It was also clear that Amber was desperate to be told what to do, clutching at all advice as an absolute.

'So you're saying I shouldn't?' Amber asked.

Margie glanced at Gareth before addressing Amber. 'No.' She shook her head. 'I'm saying that you're young, that there is currently no sign of breast cancer on any of your scans or blood tests. I'm saying this is a big decision and that you have time to make it. I'm saying that you should take that time. No decisions have to be made straight away, Amber. You might not have to do anything about it for years yet.'

Amber turned to him, a tonne of indecision in her eyes. 'What do you think?'

'I think Margie's being very sensible. She's urging caution and that you take your time. I think that's wise.'

'So you don't think I should either?'

Gareth leaned forward in his chair and placed his hands on top of Amber's fidgeting ones. 'This isn't up to me, sweetie. Or Margie. All she's saying, all we're both saying is you don't need to feel pressured into making such a huge decision right now.'

'But if I did go ahead, you'd support me, right?'

Amber's huge eyes filled with unshed tears that punched him hard in the gut. She'd looked at him with those eyes the day the oncologist had told them Catherine was terminal. Eyes that said, What the hell are we going to do?

Gareth squeezed her hands, he could not have loved this young woman any more than he did at this moment, standing at this truly horrible crossroads with her. She may not have been his from the beginning but she'd been the centre of his world from the moment she'd grinned at him with her gappy, five-year-old smile and called him Carrot.

'Of course I will, honey,' he said, and when she nodded the tears spilled from her eyes and he pulled her close, tucking her head under his chin like he used to when she was little.

'Amber,' Margie said after a few moments, having given them some time to hold each other. 'There's a really good support group here for women who deal with familial breast cancer. A lot of them are your age, facing the same kind of dilemma and questions that you are. How about I hook you up with them? You can listen to what they have to say, to their stories. It might help.'

Amber broke out of the embrace. 'Okay,' she sniffled. 'That sounds good, right?' she said, turning to look at Gareth.

He nodded. 'It sounds great.'

They walked out of the building fifteen minutes later with another appointment for a further counselling session, a bunch of pamphlets and the details for the support group Margie had recommended.

'You okay?' Gareth asked.

Amber nodded. 'Yeah. I think so. This will be good, I think,' she said, brandishing the card with the support group details.

'Yes,' he agreed. 'Fabulous that there's a meeting Saturday week too. Not that long to wait. Will you be able to get to it?'

'Yep, I should be able to.'

'You want me to see if I can swap my shift next Saturday and drive you there? I can hang around. We can grab a bite to eat after, if you want.'

She shook her head. 'Nah. I'll be fine.'

'Well, come over for tea Saturday night and tell me about it.'

'Can't,' she said. 'Carly's organised a pub crawl for Del's twenty-first.'

Gareth winced. Carly's stamina could kill an ox. 'Okay. Why don't you come around for breakfast on the Sunday after the meeting, then? Bring Carly if you want to. Sounds like you're going to need the resuscitative qualities only bacon can provide and you know I cook it better than anyone.'

Amber smiled at him and then suddenly her eyes were full of tears again as she stood on tiptoe and hugged him. 'Deal,' she whispered.

That Sunday afternoon Gareth was getting some details from his patient in cubicle three when Billie slid the curtain partially back and stepped inside.

He nodded at her, slipping on his cool, professional mask. They had only seen each other in passing since their impulsive passion the other night. The department had been busy and he was fairly certain she'd been avoiding him.

Which was fine by him.

Thinking about her every night as he drifted off to sleep, having extremely inappropriate erotic dreams about her, was hard enough. It was imperative he didn't let any thoughts of the way she'd rubbed herself against him, the way she'd kissed him the other night enter his head. They were at work and John deserved their full, undivided attention.

'Hi,' he said.

'Hi.'

She was dressed in requisite scrubs, her normal pony-tail—not one hair out of place—falling down her back. She looked like any other doctor here.

Except he wasn't treading water with any of them.

He dragged his gaze away from the gloss on her mouth. 'This is Dr Ashworth-Keyes,' Gareth said to John.

'Call me Billie,' she said, smiling at her patient.

Gareth watched John's mouth drop open. He sympathised with the guy.

'This is twenty-two-year-old John Sutton. John was kicked in the testicles during a basketball match and has what appears to be a large haematoma on his left testicle.' He looked at John. 'Dr Ashworth-Keyes will be assessing your injury.'

John's eyes practically bulged out of his head and he cast Gareth a stricken look. '*She's* going to be looking at my nuts? Don't you have a dude doctor?'

Gareth quelled an inappropriate urge to laugh as he sympathised with John again. He doubted his junk would behave itself if Billie was down there, poking and prodding, either.

'I'm sorry, Billie is it. But don't worry. She's highly quali-fied. Seen a thousand testicles,' he joked.

'Uh…okay.'

Billie saw John swallow visibly as a dull red glow stained his cheekbones. She cringed inwardly. The guy was already embarrassed and she hadn't even lifted the green surgical towel placed strategically across his lap.

This was going to be bad.

John was going to get an erection and die of complete mortification. She would then, in turn, also want the floor to swallow her whole.

No amount of saying it was a perfectly normal biological reaction was going to make this job any easier.

'Gareth?' A nurse opened the curtain a little and stuck her head in. 'Mrs Berkley's asking for you.'

Gareth sighed. 'Okay,' he said as the nurse disappeared. He looked at Billie. 'I'd better go check on her. Just yell when you're done.'

John's alarmed gaze darted to Gareth before giving Billie an extra stricken look. Billie felt for him. This had to be an embarrassing situation for him. Some guys would relish it, brag about it to their mates come Monday morning, but John didn't look like a bragger. John looked like he was already mentally trying to conjure up the least sexual things in the world.

Cane toads. Dental extraction. Burnt toast.

Billie stepped in front of Gareth, barring his exit, a forced smile on her lips. 'Can I…talk to you outside for a moment?'

Gareth frowned. 'Okay…'

Billie turned to John, her smile feeling utterly fake. 'We'll be right back.'

They stepped outside the curtain and Gareth pulled it closed. The department was busy and people bustled around them. Billie waited for a nurse to pass before she started. 'You can't leave me in there with him,' she said, her voice low. 'You have to stay.'

Gareth blinked. 'What? Why?'

'Because!' Her voice dropped. 'The guy is clearly worried that…' She switched to a whisper, '*Things* are going to happen as soon as I examine him, and I'd rather save him and myself the embarrassment.'

'The guy's got a black and blue testicle,' Gareth whispered in reply. 'I don't think *anything's* going to happening down there any time soon.'

'Maybe. But the point is, *he* thinks it will,' she murmured, still keeping her voice hushed but not whispering any longer.

'And how is me being in there with you going to help?'

'Because you're a *guy*. You can distract him with guy things.'

He quirked his eyebrow. 'Guy things?'

'Yes. You know. Beer and football and…'

Billie wasn't sure what men talked about. The men in her family talked about the latest surgical technique. She didn't think that was what John needed to hear, considering he was probably going to be under a surgeon's knife by night's end.

'…mountain climbing.'

Gareth laughed. Beer and football he could manage. Everest not so much. 'Mountain climbing?'

His low chuckle was equal parts sexy and irritating and Billie glared at him. 'Sporty stuff.'

Gareth shoved his hands on his hips. 'And what would you do if I wasn't here?'

'I'd find another male on staff to accompany me.'

'And what would happen if there were only female staff on?'

'Then, of course, I'd do it myself,' Billie said. 'But you *are* here and I don't have to. Now, can you please help a fellow male out and distract him for me?'

'With all my mountain-climbing stories?'

Billie rolled her eyes. 'With whatever you like.'

'Okay. But only if you help me with Mrs Berkley after.'

She narrowed her eyes. 'What's wrong with Mrs Berkley?'

'She's an eighty-four-year-old PFO with a fractured wrist.'

Billie frowned. 'PFO?'

'Pissed and fell over.'

'I *know* what it means, Gareth,' she said. She may have only have been in the ER for a couple of weeks but she'd picked up the vernacular quickly.

Medicine was full of acronyms. Both official and unofficial. 'But…eighty-four?'

He grinned. 'Yup.'

'Do I want to know what she was doing?'

'I believe it was the Chicken Dance at her great-grand-son's wedding.'

Billie whistled. 'Go, Mrs Berkley.'

'Easy for you to say. She's a little high and...' Gareth searched for the right word and smiled as their conversation from the other night came back to him. 'Grabby.'

Billie regarded him for a moment as he plunged her straight back into the middle of that night, their kiss, his erection pressing hard and urgent at the juncture of her thighs.

Crap.

She'd been doing just fine pretending it hadn't happened but suddenly she was there again—the firelight, the confidences, the wine.

'Please, Billie.'

Billie dragged herself out of the sexual morass. Gareth looked more than a little desperate and it was almost comical to see such an experienced nurse worried about a little old lady. 'Since when did the big military guy have problems fending off a sweet old lady with a broken wrist?'

'I don't have a problem,' he said firmly. 'I'd just rather have a female member of staff there while she's not in her right mind. Between the alcohol and the happy juice the ambos gave her, she's not quite herself.'

Billie laughed at the picture Gareth was creating. 'Well, at least she's not feeling anything.'

'Oh, she's not feeling a thing. She's singing sea shanties.'

'She sounds a hoot.' Billie grinned.

'A hoot with wandering hands.'

Billie laughed again. She couldn't blame Mrs Berkley. Gareth was utterly grab-worthy. 'Okay, fine.' She checked her watch. 'John first then the irrepressible Mrs Berkley.'

'Deal,' he said, as he pulled back the curtain and they both trooped back in.

'Right, John,' Billie said, approaching the nervous patient briskly, professionally, reaching for some gloves that were in a dispenser attached to the wall behind the gurney and quickly snapping them on. 'Let's see what you've done to yourself.'

As she pulled up the corner of the green towel she heard Gareth say, 'So, done any mountain climbing, John?' and it took all her willpower not to laugh.

The urge died quickly as the extent of John's bruising was revealed. Gareth was right—it was black and blue. And very, very swollen. She winced.

'He's had some pain relief?' she asked.

Gareth nodded. 'Morphine.'

She looked at John, who was looking anywhere but at her. 'How's the pain?'

'It's better,' he said, the blush darkening on his cheeks as he spoke to a spot just beyond her ear.

'Okay, good, but I'm sorry…I have to have a feel, okay?'

John swallowed. 'Okay.'

Billie carried out the examination as gently as she could, feeling both testicles methodically. Gareth prattled on about Sherpas and carabineers. She flipped the towel back over when she was done and stripped off her gloves.

'Right. We're going to get the surgical doctor on call to come and see you but I think you've got yourself a nasty haematoma down there that'll need to be evacuated.'

John, a nice colour of beetroot now, nodded, looking at his toes. 'The surgical doctor, is it a…woman?'

Billie bit the inside of her cheek. It was heartening if somewhat foolish to meet a guy who was more concerned about the sex of the doctor than the fact his testicle looked like a battered plum.

She patted his foot. 'Dr Yates is very much male.'

John's sigh of relief was audible.

CHAPTER THIRTEEN

'Ah, there you are, you gorgeous young man.' The elderly woman lying on the exam table located in the middle of the room had a twinkle in her eyes as she waggled her fingers at Gareth and Billie almost laughed out loud at her greeting. 'I thought you'd skipped out on me.'

'Me? Skip out on you, Mrs Berkley?' Gareth murmured, and Billie blinked at the low, easy, flirty tone to his voice. 'Never.'

'Oh, and you've bought a pretty young woman with you.' Mrs Berkley beamed at Billie. 'Come in, my dear.' She gestured with her good arm. 'My goodness, how *do* you young people get things done around here with so much to distract you?'

He glanced at Billie. Their gazes locked and her breath hitched for a second.

'It's a challenge, Mrs B., I can't deny that,' Gareth said, before switching his attention to the patient, sitting himself down on the stool beside the table and swinging slightly from side to side.

Mrs B. cackled merrily. 'I can imagine. I remember when me and my Ted were going around. Couldn't pass each other without wanting to tear each other's clothes off.'

Billie blinked at the frank admission and Gareth stopped swivelling on the stool as the room filled with a pregnant silence.

'Hah.' The octogenarian cracked up again. 'That shocked the cotton socks off you, didn't it? What, you think you young people invented sex?'

Gareth recovered quite quickly. 'Absolutely not, and I thank you and your generation most earnestly for your pioneering ways.'

Mrs B. grinned from ear to ear. 'You're welcome,' she said, her hand covering Gareth's and giving it a pat. 'I could tell you some stories that would make you blush right to the roots of your hair.'

Billie's mind boggled but Gareth had her measure. 'I don't embarrass easily, Mrs B. We nurses aren't prone to being shocked.'

Billie was pleased Gareth wasn't shocked because she had to admit to feeling just the tiniest bit so. She didn't know if Mrs B. was always this outrageous or if it was the combination of alcohol and drugs but Billie wasn't used to such freeness of expression *in eighty-year-olds*.

But it appeared Mrs Berkley was on a roll. The older woman gave Gareth a secretive smile and tapped the side of her nose three times. 'I still reckon I could teach you a thing or two, young man.'

Gareth, looking completely unconcerned by the flirting, grinned and said, 'I'll bet you could.'

Mrs B. turned her eyes on Billie. 'Isn't he marvellous, dear? I mean, really, do they have those nudie calendars for male nurses...you know, like they do for the firefighters? This young man could be the centrefold.'

Now Billie really was at a loss for words and not just because they'd been uttered by a great-grandmother. The illicit thought of Gareth stripped nude made her lose her train of thought.

She glanced at Gareth, who was looking at her with a quirked eyebrow. 'Yes,' he mused. 'Why don't we do calendars?'

Billie really felt like she'd leapt into an alternate universe.

She needed to get them out of this bizarre conversation immediately. Why was Gareth encouraging her? Hadn't he asked her in here to defend his honour?

'Inappropriate perhaps?' she said, smiling sweetly.

Mrs B. nudged Gareth and said in a stage whisper they could probably hear out in the ambulance bay, 'Ooh. She's a bit of a spoilsport, that one.'

Gareth, his gaze still locked with hers, a small smile playing on his lips, nodded. 'Yes, she is.'

Billie almost choked on his statement. She wasn't going to stand by and be defamed when nothing could be further than the truth. 'Don't listen to a word he says, Mrs Berkley. The only spoilsport around here is Gareth.'

She raised an eyebrow back at him. It hadn't been her who had knocked him back. *Twice.* He had the good grace to look away.

'Right,' he said, turning back to his patient. 'Let's get this cast on, shall we? A nice light fibreglass one for you today.'

'Ooh, can I have a purple one?' Mrs Berkley asked. 'My great-granddaughter Kahlia had one last year.' She glanced at Billie. 'It looked very groovy.'

Gareth nodded. They had a selection of colours for paediatric patients so why not? 'Purple it is. Let me get set up.'

She beamed at him and patted his cheek. 'Such a good boy.'

Gareth smiled and extracted himself. He rummaged through the supply cupboard and found some rolls of purple. 'Can I help?' Billie asked, appearing at his elbow.

'Sure. Fill this halfway,' he said, thrusting a stainless-steel basin at her.

'What are you doing?' she whispered under her breath as she took it. 'Why am I here if you keep encouraging her?'

'Because I just spent twenty minutes talking to a very confused guy about hiking boots and grappling hooks.'

She rolled her eyes. 'You didn't have to talk to him about mountain climbing and you know it.'

Gareth grinned at her. 'Now, where would the fun have been in that?' He nodded his head to the right. 'Sink over there.'

A few minutes later they were set up. Gareth had the rolls of plaster soaking in the basin that had been set on a trolley, and he was sitting back on his stool, pulled in close to the table. Billie was sitting on the other side of Mrs Berkley, also on a stool.

He positioned her arm correctly and started to apply the padded underlay. His hair flopped forward as he worked his way up to her elbow and Mrs Berkley reached out her unbroken hand and pushed it back off his forehead.

Gareth looked up at her, startled. 'I miss running my hands through a man's hair,' she said wistfully.

'Okay, Mrs B.,' Billie said, taking the older woman's hand and bringing her arm back down beside her. She intertwined her fingers with the patient's and gave the gnarled old hand a squeeze. 'How about we let Gareth finish his job?'

'Yes, of course, dear,' Mrs Berkley said, and tutted to herself a couple of times. 'I guess I'm probably making a bit of an old fool of myself. I just so rarely get to hang out with younger people these days.'

Billie squeezed her hand again. 'Of course not,' she murmured. 'You're just keeping Gareth on his toes.' She glanced across at him. 'Men need that.'

'Damn straight,' Mrs Berkley hooted, her crinkly face splitting into a hundred different ravines, deep and beautiful.

Once the padding was in situ Gareth plunged his gloved hand into the basin and removed the first roll. 'You sure about purple?' he asked.

Mrs Berkley nodded her head enthusiastically. 'Quite.'

He squeezed the roll out gently, removing the excess water, and started applying the first layer. 'You should ask this young lady out,' Mrs Berkley said, out of the blue.

Billie's alarmed gaze met Gareth's across the top of their

patient. Gareth returned his to the job at hand, but not before murmuring, 'You don't say?'

'Oh, yes.' Mrs Berkley nodded. 'You'd look good together. Make *beautiful* babies. Her hair and complexion, your eyes and strapping physique. Perfect.'

'But we work together, Mrs B. You know they say you should never mix business with pleasure.'

Mrs Berkley snorted. 'What a load of old tosh. What do *they* know? They are the cat's mother. And what do cats have to do with it?'

Billie frowned. What indeed? she thought as she tried to follow the muddled ponderings. But somehow in this very strange conversation nothing seemed too bizarre.

'What do you reckon, Billie? You fancy a date?'

Mrs Berkley gave a horrified gasp. 'Young man, that is no way to ask a young lady out. Where are your manners? Now, do it again. Properly this time!'

Billie glanced at Gareth, who was looking suitably chastised, and she bit down on her lip to stop laughing.

'You do know how to ask, don't you?' Mrs Berkley said, clearly not done with her disapproval.

'To be honest,' Gareth said, the smile slipping from his face, 'it's been a while for me.'

A shiver wormed its way up Billie's spine at Gareth's sudden grimness. Been a while since what? He'd gone on a date? It certainly hadn't been a while since he'd kissed a woman—she could attest to that. Or did he mean it had been a while since he'd taken a woman to bed?

Had he slept with anyone since his wife had died?

'You say,' Mrs Berkley said in a voice that was half imperious, half exasperated, '"Would you do me the honour of accompanying me to dinner?" Or wherever you're going.'

His patient's disgust brought Gareth back from the edge of the familiar darkness that had overwhelmed him for a long time. He laughed.

Mrs B. was so affronted it was hard not to.

'Of course, you're right, Mrs B.' He unwound the last of the first roll then looked across at Billie as he picked up the second. 'Willamina Ashworth-Keyes, will you do me the honour of having a drink with me after work tonight?'

His blue eyes sparkled playfully, the shadows she'd seen there moments ago banished, making it hard for Billie to ascertain if he was serious or just humouring Mrs Berkley. It worked anyway as the octogenarian nodded approvingly.

'Good. Now you…' she looked at Billie '…say, "Why, thank you, I'd be delighted to have a drink with you after work tonight."'

Billie glanced at Gareth, who gave her an encouraging little wink before returning to the cast. So they were just humouring their patient, then…?

Disappointment trickled down her spine.

'Why…thank you, Gareth Stapleton,' she said, forcing an equally light tone to her voice. 'I'd be delighted to have a drink with you after work tonight.'

He chuckled as he worked and Billie's disappointment grew. Mrs Berkley clapped. 'There, see. Perfect. My work here is done.'

'And so,' Gareth announced as he unrolled the last of the roll, smoothing the end down thoroughly, 'is mine. There you go.' He stood. 'All pretty in purple.'

Mrs Berkley looked at Gareth's handiwork. 'I love it,' she said, grinning.

'Another happy customer,' he said, smiling at Mrs Berkley with such genuine affection it took Billie's breath away. Was there nothing the man couldn't do? Pull heart-attack victims out of wrecks, run an emergency room with military efficiency, while calming freaked out residents *and* charm little old ladies.

'Now, let's get you up and outside for a while. You'll need to stick around for an hour or so in case there's swelling, then you can be on your way.'

'Right you are,' Mrs Berkley said, as Gareth ushered her

into a wheelchair. 'Hand me my bag, will you, dear?' she asked Billie. 'I'll text my granddaughter to come and get me in an hour.'

Billie handed Mrs Berkley her handbag, still trying to wrap her head around an eighty-four-year-old with a smartphone. Gareth flipped the brake off with his foot. 'Hold tight,' he said.

'It was nice meeting you, Mrs B.,' Billie said, as the wheelchair drew level with her. 'Maybe no more chicken dancing for a while.'

Mrs Berkley smiled at her. 'I'm old, my dear. I'm going to chicken dance while I can.' She patted Billy's hand. 'Gotta make hay before those chickens hatch. Enjoy your date.'

Gareth grinned and winked, pushing the chair past her before Billie had a sensible reply. She watched them go, Mrs Berkley saying, 'I don't suppose you could round me up a cuppa, could you, dear? I'm desperate for one,' as Gareth pushed her down the corridor.

His deep 'Of course I can, anything for you, Mrs B.,' as they disappeared from sight was typical Gareth. From CPR to cups of tea, he was a regular knight in shining armour.

He'd certainly saved her ass more than once.

CHAPTER FOURTEEN

A FEW HOURS LATER, Billie changed out of her scrubs in the female locker room. It had been a long day and her feet were killing her. She needed a hot shower, a glass of wine and her bed. Slipping into her trendy, buckle-laden boots, she threw her Italian leather jacket over her arm, grabbed her bag and headed out.

Gareth was lounging against the opposite wall when she opened the door. He was wearing jeans that looked old and worn and soft as butter, some kind of duffle coat and a smile. The coat was open to reveal a snug-fitting shirt and he looked all warm and rugged and just a little bit wild, like he was about to throw his leg over a motorbike. Billie had to grind her heels into the ground to stop herself from slipping her arms inside his coat and snuggling into the broad expanse of his chest.

'I thought you were never coming out,' he said, as he pushed off the wall and moved closer.

'Sorry,' she said, puzzled. 'Did I miss signing something?'

'Nah.' He indicated that she should walk and they fell into step. 'Mrs B. just rang to make sure that I was collecting you for our date.'

Billie stopped for a moment. 'She did?'

He grinned and nodded, also stopping. 'She did.'

'Wow,' Billie murmured, as they commenced walking again, conscious of Gareth's arm casually brushing hers.

'I'm surprised she can even remember through all that happy juice.'

'I have a feeling that Mrs B. doesn't miss much at all.'

Billie laughed. 'I think you may be right.'

They got to the end of the corridor and Billie went to turn right for the lifts and the car park.

'Hey, where are you going?' Gareth asked. 'What about our date?'

Billie's breath caught in her throat. He was looking at her with a tease in those blue eyes and something else, something very *frank*. His promise to Elvis her brains out echoed around her head but that had been a few days ago and nothing he'd done since had indicated that the event was likely to happen, much less imminently.

'Oh...I didn't think that was real,' she stalled.

He shrugged. 'It wasn't but...I'm pretty sure Mrs B. has this place bugged and when she rings tomorrow looking for me—and she *assures* me she's going to—I'll be able to put my hand on my heart and tell her I was the epitome of a gentleman.'

Billie didn't think he looked remotely gentlemanly right now. He looked all whiskery and hunky and she could suddenly picture him beneath the rotors of a chopper, accepting a wounded soldier. She certainly didn't want him to act all gentlemanly. She wanted him to push her against the wall in the deserted corridor and kiss her until she didn't have any breath left in her chest.

She wanted a quick, hard military incursion.

Billie blushed and covered her embarrassingly real fantasy with a spot of mocking. 'You? *You're* frightened of a little old lady.'

'*That* little old lady?' Gareth grinned. 'Hell, yeah. What do you say? A quick drink at Oscar's for Mrs B.'s sake?'

Billie knew she should say no. But Gareth was hard to resist when he was being all charming and he-man. And who was she to disappoint an octogenarian?

'Okay, sure. But I expect you to be on your very best behaviour or I'll tell Mrs Berkley.'

'Yes, ma'am,' he murmured, saluting her, and Billie's pulse just about ratcheted off the scale.

Billie was very pleased as they entered Oscar's that she'd decided to dress nicely that morning. She was wearing her designer jeans and a fluffy-on-the-outside, fleecy-on-the-inside zip-up jumper that pulled nicely across her breasts and showed off a decent hint of cleavage.

She knew that this was just them humouring an old woman but it didn't hurt to be looking her best either.

Gareth held out a chair for her and Billie smiled. 'Very gallant,' she murmured. 'Keep this up and I'll expect you to throw your cloak over a puddle for me.'

Gareth grinned. 'Sorry, I'm fresh out of cloaks. But I will buy you a drink. Wine?'

Billie nodded. 'Red.'

She watched him walk away. He'd removed his jacket and the way his jeans hung to the long, lazy stride of his legs should have been illegal. Billie felt a little flutter in her chest. They weren't even on a real date and Gareth was already doing better than any other man she'd been out with.

She watched him laughing with the guy behind the bar as he picked up their drinks and brought them over. Everything seemed easy with him. From his laid-back chuckle to the looseness of his stride, to the slow spread of his lazy grin.

'Baz recommends the Merlot, apparently,' he said as he placed the glass of ruby liquid in front of her.

Billie smiled. Of course he knew the name of the guy behind the bar—Gareth knew everyone. He sat and raised his glass towards her. 'To Mrs Berkley,' he said, smiling as they clinked their glasses.

Some froth from Gareth's beer clung to his top lip and Billie had to drag her gaze away from it as she groped around for a distraction. 'So...what now?' she asked.

'Well, I guess we should do that getting-to-know-you stuff that dates are for.'

Billie gave a half-laugh. 'You already know about my dead sister, my fragile mother, my pompous father, my inability to deny them anything and my pathological dislike of gore. I know about your wife, your stepdaughter, the way you handle yourself in an emergency and what you've been doing for the last decade or so. What else is there to know?'

Gareth laughed. That was a very good question. 'We have done the big stuff, haven't we?'

He was sure there was more for both of them—hell, they both had a tonne of baggage. But Gareth wasn't in the mood for heavy tonight. Suddenly he wanted to know the little stuff.

'What's your favourite colour?'

Billie blinked. 'My favourite colour?'

'Sure. Let's do the pop-quiz version.'

Okay…that could be fun. 'Um…yellow,' she said. 'What's yours? No…hang on, let me guess…khaki?'

Gareth laughed. 'Ha. Funny girl. Definitely not.' He looked at her hair then back at her. 'Chestnut,' he said, taking a sip of his beer.

Billie's pulse skipped a beat.

He took another swig of his beer, taking care this time to remove any errant foam, for which Billie was exceedingly grateful. 'Favourite food,' he said.

'Jam on toast.'

Gareth threw back his head and laughed. '*That's* your favourite food?'

Billie raised an eyebrow at him. 'You got a problem with that?'

'Nope. Just find it hard to believe that Willamina Ashworth-Keyes eats jam on toast.'

'Well, *she* doesn't. But plain old Billie Keyes loves it!' She took a mouthful of her wine. 'I suppose yours is caviar? No, wait…quiche!'

He grinned at her deliberate goading. 'A steak. Big, thick and juicy.'

'How very tough guy of you.'

Gareth laughed some more. 'You don't like tough guys?'

Billie's gaze wandered to where the hem of his sleeve brushed his biceps. She raised her eyes to his face and warmth flooded her cheeks. She'd had no experience of tough guys whatsoever. The men she'd been with had been cultured and urbane.

'I'm liking them more and more.'

Their gazes locked for long moments then Gareth smiled. 'You're good for my ego.'

Billie pulse fluttered as she dragged herself back from the compelling blueness of his eyes and reminded herself this wasn't a real date. 'Well…we won't tell Mrs B. that.'

Gareth found himself laughing again. It felt good to talk and laugh with a woman—really good. It had been a long time since he felt this *all over* good and he was suddenly overwhelmed by how easy it was.

Billie put him at ease.

When she wasn't tying him in knots.

His smiled faded a little as he contemplated the implications. 'I like you, Willamina Ashworth-Keyes.'

Everything stilled inside Billie as the sudden, serious admission fell from his lips. She didn't know what to say but she knew she felt the same way. 'I like you too, Gareth Stapleton.'

The bar noises faded into the background as they stared at each other, their drinks forgotten in front of them.

'Hey, guys, Gareth and Billie are here.'

The words yanked them out of their little bubble and they turned to see a bunch of emergency nurses heading their way.

'Uh-oh,' Gareth said. 'Date's over.'

Billie nodded. 'Leave this bit out when you speak to Mrs B. tomorrow.'

Gareth smiled. 'Good idea.'

And then they were being swamped with company as

half a dozen colleagues descended and Billie gave herself up to the mayhem.

Because it wasn't a real date anyway.

The following Saturday, Gareth watched Billie through a crack in cubicle four's curtain. He was supposed to be doing paperwork so he could finish up and get out of there but his gaze continued to be drawn to her.

She was examining a nasty cellulitic arm from an infected scratch. She said something to her patient, a fifty-two-year-old male, and he laughed. Billie laughed with him and he admired the effortless way she put people at ease.

They responded to her.

And Gareth knew that patients who liked and trusted the doctors they saw were more likely to take their advice.

He liked seeing her at ease. It was her natural habitat and a far cry from the woman she became when confronted with the rawness of a medical emergency. There was something compelling about her. She looked cool and confident. Sure of herself.

And that was very, very sexy.

He'd tried hard not to dwell on their *date* this past week and had failed miserably. It seemed to be the only thing he *had* thought about and he was thinking about it again now as she charmed her patient. The teasing and the banter had been fun and he realised he wanted to see more of her.

Sure, there were a lot of reasons why seeing her outside work was dumb. They both knew that. But right from the beginning there'd been an inevitability about them, he'd felt it and so had she. Hell, he'd told her that night at her place that something would happen between them sooner or later.

And the time for fighting it was over.

He wanted to see her, touch her, kiss her. He didn't want to keep his distance, push her away again. He wanted her in his bed. For however long it lasted.

And he hadn't felt this way since Catherine.

So forget the rest of it.

Billie glanced up and Gareth realised he'd been caught staring. Their gazes held for a long moment before she turned back and said something to her patient, and Gareth felt as if his chest wall had just been released from a vice.

When she strode towards him a minute later, he was still recovering.

'Shouldn't you have knocked off by now?' she said, as she took the chair beside him at the work station, her voice casual but he could tell she was being deliberately so.

'Yep,' Gareth said. 'Just finishing up some charting.'

'Ah,' she murmured, as she opened the chart in front of her, 'the never-ending paperwork.'

He laughed. 'Yes.' They continued their charting in silence for a moment. Gareth glanced sideways at her, briefly admiring her neat handwriting. They were the only two at the work station for now. 'I think we should go on a proper date,' he said.

She looked up and her ponytail swished to the side. She frowned at him, which emphasised her freckles. 'R-really?'

Gareth nodded. 'Yes.'

Her throat bobbed and his gaze followed the tantalising movement. 'When?'

'Tonight?' Why not. *Seize the day.*

There was a drawn-out silence as she regarded him solemnly. 'There seem to be a lot of reasons why we shouldn't.'

She was looking at him as if she was remembering the last two times she'd tried to reach out to him and he'd rejected her. 'Yes, there are.' He nodded. 'But I don't care any more.'

Gareth took her nervous swallow as a good sign. A nurse swished past the desk and Billie faked interest in the chart until they were alone again.

'Could I take a raincheck?' she asked, lifting her gaze from the chart. 'I'm not off for a couple of hours yet and I'm beat. The thought of having to go home and get dressed up and go out...'

Gareth tried really hard *not* to think about her getting dressed up. For him. 'That's okay. Just come to my place straight from work. I'll cook you dinner and you don't have to get dressed up.'

Also, if he didn't do this now, he was frightened he'd chicken out altogether. That common sense would win out.

'Oh.' Billie looked back at the chart again and Gareth wasn't sure if that was a good thing or a bad thing. Was she weighing up the pros and cons or freaking out?

When she lifted her eyes there was a directness to her gaze that was utterly compelling. 'Thank you. I'd love to.'

Gareth hadn't realised how much had been mentally riding on her acceptance until she'd uttered it and he sagged a little.

'Can I bring something?' she asked, her gaze unwavering. 'Beer, wine, dessert?' She looked around surreptitiously and lowered her voice. 'Condoms?'

Gareth blinked but their gazes still held. She wanted to know the lie of the land—he could understand that. He shook his head. 'I'm good. For *everything*.'

Her mouth quirking up at the side was the only indication that they were talking about something they probably shouldn't have been, considering where they were. And it added to the anticipation of the moment.

'In that case, I look forward to it very much, thank you,' she murmured.

Gareth's mouth quirked up too. 'My pleasure.'

She held his gaze for a little longer. 'I hope so,' she said, then returned her attention to the chart.

CHAPTER FIFTEEN

BILLIE WAS NERVOUS when she pulled up at Gareth's just after eight-thirty. She couldn't quite believe how up front she'd been about her expectations of this night and she cringed a little now, thinking about it.

But she was a grown woman, a fully qualified doctor, for crying out loud—she knew what she wanted and she wasn't ashamed to ask for it. It was past time for them to stop beating around the bush. This wasn't some fake date for the sake of an old lady.

This was the real thing.

And there was something between her and Gareth. She'd felt the pull from the beginning and that hadn't lessened. Every time she looked at him, every time he was near she felt it and she knew he did too.

Okay, she had a lot going on in her life at the moment. She was struggling with decisions in her life she didn't feel she had any control over. But she didn't care about that right now because she did have control over this. Tonight she needed to be with him and that's all she cared about.

And Gareth, thankfully, had agreed.

Billie's breath misted into the air as she climbed the five stairs and put her foot on the wide veranda that continued all the way in both directions, typical of the old Queenslander style of architecture.

She rapped on the door, wishing again she'd thought to

wear something a little more elegant to work this morning instead of a pair of track pants, a turtleneck sweater and her seen-better-days college jumper.

Yes, it had been freezing, as it was now, but she could have at least worn something more along the lines of what she'd worn the day they'd ended up on their fake date.

She wasn't even wearing matching underwear.

Sure, he'd seen her looking worse—in plain baggy scrubs at half past stupid o'clock in the morning, tired and cold and hungry and feeling like death—but he'd also seen her in her best sparkly cocktail dress with full make-up and hair in curls.

Of course, she'd thrown up on him then too so maybe that didn't count…

Billie heard footsteps and she could see his shape coming towards her in the glass side panes of the door. Her pulse sped up. The light flicked on overhead and she quickly pulled her hair out from the constraints of her standard workwear ponytail and fluffed it a little as the door opened.

'Hi,' Gareth murmured, a smile tugging at the corners of his mouth.

He was wearing jeans and a long-sleeved button-up shirt, left undone at the neck, and his hair was damp. He looked so good and clean and warm and laid-back, casual sexy, she couldn't decide if she wanted to snuggle him or jump him.

'Hi,' she said, suddenly realising she was staring.

They didn't say anything or do anything for a few moments. Gareth just looked at her and Billie's stomach twisted in a knot.

'You look good,' he murmured.

Billie laughed then because she knew good was stretching it. 'It's okay. You don't have compliment me,' she said. 'Trust me, I'm a sure thing.'

He shook his head, slid his hand onto her hip and pulled her in close to him, bringing his mouth to within millimetres of hers, hovering it oh-so-close. So close she could feel the warmth of his breath and smell the mint of his toothpaste.

'You look good,' he repeated, his husky voice reaching inside, plucking at the fibres of her belly deep and low.

Then he dropped his mouth to hers and Billie felt the impact to her system like a lightning bolt. She moaned as he opened his mouth over hers and demanded she do the same. And she did. He urged her body closer and she went.

She wrapped her arms around his neck, flattened her breasts against his chest, aligned her pelvis with his and then somehow she was inside and the door was shut and a warm wall was hard behind her and he was hard in front of her and he groaned her name like it was torn from the depth of his soul and she never wanted to let him go.

And when he broke the kiss off she mewed in protest, their breathing harsh in the sudden silence.

'Sorry,' he murmured, pulling away slightly to look at her. 'I promised myself I'd wait but I've been fantasising about doing that for hours.'

Billie shrugged. His lips were wet from her mouth and she wanted them back on hers again. 'Don't stop on my behalf.'

'Oh, no, if I don't stop now I won't stop at all and what would Mrs Berkley think if I invited a young lady to dinner and then she didn't get any?'

Billie laughed. 'I think she'd disapprove. I'd think she'd think you quite ungentlemanly.'

He grinned. 'Me too.' He dropped his hands from her hips and took a reluctant step back. 'Come on, I've even cooked for you.' He held out his hand and she took it. 'I hope you're hungry.'

'*Very*,' she murmured, as he led the way through the house, his completely asexual touch doing funny things to her legs anyway.

He chuckled at her emphasis, leaving her in no doubt he knew she wasn't talking about food. 'I made a basil and cherry-tomato pasta.'

They entered the kitchen. 'Glass of wine?'

'Yes, please.' If he was determined that they eat first then she was going to need to do something with her hands other than putting them all over him.

'Take a seat,' he said, gesturing to the stools along the far side of the wide central kitchen bench.

'This is a nice place,' she said, looking up at what she figured had to be a twelve-foot ceiling. That, combined with the panelled walls and the wraparound veranda, confirmed its architectural heritage.

'Yes,' Gareth, said as he poured a glass of red wine for her and cracked the lid of a beer for himself. 'It's not mine, I'm just house-sitting, but I believe it's almost one hundred years old. The owners had it moved from a homestead out west.'

'You're house-sitting? For friends?'

Gareth shook his head as he handed over her glass of wine. 'No. It's what I do. I house-sit for people.'

'You don't have a…permanent home?'

'Nope,' Gareth said, as he went and checked the food on the stove. 'I sold our house a couple of years after Catherine died, when Amber headed to uni, so I could put half of it in trust for her.'

'Oh.'

He turned and lounged against the oven. His jeans pulled tight against his thighs as he casually sipped his beer. He looked calm and comfortable in his skin and that cranked the sexy up another notch.

Billie was thankful there was a bench separating them.

'Catherine didn't really have anything of monetary value to leave Amber. Only what we had together, like the house and cars. And I wanted Amber to be able to have a legacy from her mother, something that could help her get a good start in life when she was ready.'

'So you sold your house?'

Gareth shook his head. 'It was our house. And, besides, it felt empty, not like a home any more. Catherine was gone and Amber was at college. Without them to fill it up it was just four walls and a roof.'

He stared into his drink for long moments, suddenly sombre, and Billie was pleased anew for the bench separating them. She wanted to go to him. Go to him, comfort him.

Which would probably embarrass the hell out of him. And herself. But the urge was there nonetheless.

'The house sold much faster than I'd anticipated so I was going to rent until I found something, but at the same time a friend of mine was going away for a few months and asked if I wanted to house-sit and it sort of snowballed from there. I'm with an agency now and I haven't been without a place to stay since. These owners have moved to Switzerland for a year.'

Billie's heart broke a little for Gareth. She loved her house—the one thing she'd accomplished without any help from her parents after she'd refused their monetary assistance.

Because she'd wanted to do it herself but mostly because of the guilt strings that came attached.

She loved how it grounded her. How she walked into it after a shift and it felt familiar and right, it felt like a home. She couldn't imagine walking into her house and it not feeling like a home any more.

She couldn't imagine walking away from it.

'Isn't it strange, having nowhere to call your own? Eating in someone else's kitchen, sitting on someone else's couch, sleeping in someone else's bed'

'Nah. I'm used to moving around from my years in the military. It feels right.'

'So you'll never get your own place again?'

He shook his head. 'I will…one day, I guess. The money's there. I could have done it at any point. But I liked the gypsy lifestyle. I've felt very…cast adrift these last few years, I guess…so this suits me for now.'

Billie sipped her wine. 'And how does Amber feel about that?'

'Amber has her own life. As she should. And she has financial security that she wouldn't have if I was still in the house. And as long as there's a spare bed for her when she needs it, she doesn't care where I live.'

'She sounds like an extraordinary young woman.'

'Yes.' He nodded. 'She is. Considering what she's been through.'

'She sounds like she's lucky to have you.'

Gareth shook his head. 'No. *I'm* lucky to have *her*.'

Billie's throat clogged with emotion. She'd never met a man like Gareth. A man who was unashamedly frank about his feelings, who had his priorities straight. She thought about her own father, who'd never told her how lucky he was to have her. He *had* told her *frequently* how lucky she was to have him, though.

His experience, his influence, his name.

He'd never even cried at Jessica's funeral.

'I hope you tell her that,' Billie murmured.

'Yep, as often as I can.' He smiled at her. 'I'll serve up.'

Gareth took their plates through to the formal dining room and set them down at the large table that seated twelve.

'Wow,' Billie said, looking above her at the imposing chandelier. 'Do you eat in here?'

'Nah, I usually eat in the lounge room in front of the telly; I like to catch up on the news but I figured an Ashworth-Keyes is used to formal dining,' he teased.

Billie grimaced. She *had* grown up with formal dining. In fact, they'd had a chandelier quite similar to this one.

'I vote for the lounge,' she said. 'This Ashworth-Keyes prefers relaxed and casual.'

Gareth's gaze met and held hers for a brief moment. He smiled at her and her breath hitched. 'There is nothing casual about you.'

Billie blushed. She didn't know what he meant by that exactly. Did he mean that she was too serious, too much of a mess? Or did he mean she wasn't going to be casual in his life?

She looked down to hide her confusion, her daggy jumper staring back at her. 'I don't know,' she said, looking back at him. 'I'm not exactly dressed for the opera.'

He grinned as he picked up the plates. 'All the better to undress you.'

Billie's insides quivered as she followed.

Gareth put some music on low and they chatted as they ate. Billie seemed stilted at first—not that he could blame her after his blatant statement of intent in the dining room—but she soon warmed up.

Conversation quickly drifted to his time in the military and they talked long after they'd set their bowls aside. He told her a bit about his postings and she asked him about the things he'd seen that had given him faith in the human race.

The question surprised him. Most people wanted to know the gory details. But he guessed, given Billie's abhorrence of gore, she was positioned to ask an atypical question.

'Was it hard to leave?' she asked.

Gareth shook his head. 'I loved being in the military. Putting on that uniform made me feel proud and worthy. It took me places and gave me opportunities to make a difference I wouldn't have had otherwise, but I was away from home a lot and if someone had told me that I was going to lose Catherine after only ten years together, I would have ditched the military in an instant and spent every one of those years by her side. We thought we'd have decades.'

Billie slid her hand onto his. 'Life's shorter than we think sometimes,' she whispered.

Gareth glanced at her. Moisture shimmered in her eyes. Was she thinking about her sister? 'I'm never making that mistake again,' he said, turning his hand over, her fingers automatically interlocking with his.

'She didn't mind you being away so much?' Billie asked.

'No. She knew how much I loved my job and Catherine was the most self-reliant woman I'd ever met. She'd been a single mother for five years, she could look after herself and she didn't mind being on her own.'

'She sounds great.'

Gareth nodded. 'You would have liked her.' He looked down at their hands. '*She* would have liked you.' The silence grew between them and Gareth glanced up. Billie looked wistful and a little sad. 'Sorry… God…' He shook his head. 'Way to kill a mood…talk incessantly about your dead wife.'

She laughed then. 'No, it's fine. I don't mind. I wish I could talk more about Jess. But she's such a taboo topic at home.'

'It's too painful for your parents still?'

'Yes,' Billie said. 'Mum can't even bear to hear her name uttered. And I think Dad feels this sense of…failure. My father comes from a long line of successful, ground-breaking surgeons; everything the Ashworth-Keyes clan have ever attempted has ended in success. And they like to talk about their successes, celebrate them. They don't talk about their failures. And I think he feels like he failed with Jess most of all.'

'I'm sorry,' Gareth said.

She shrugged. 'It is what it is.'

Gareth put his arm around her and snuggled her into the crook of his shoulder. Her head fitted under his chin, the silky strands of her hair brushing his skin. Their legs were already stretched out in front of them, their bare feet propped on the coffee table. He inched his foot closer to hers and rubbed it gently against her.

'What *was* she like?' he asked, as he absently dropped a kiss on the top of her head.

Billie didn't answer for a while and he could feel the tension across her shoulders as if the memories had been kept inside for so long it was taking an effort to drag them out and dust them off. But he didn't mind waiting. The music was nice and she was snuggled in close and he knew the benefits of talking about those you'd loved and lost.

He and Amber often talked about Catherine.

'She had this mad laugh,' Billie said after a while. 'Like… really loud…*honking*, my father called it. He always thought Jess did it deliberately to annoy him.'

'And did she?'

'No. Well…maybe she took some pleasure in emphasising it.'

He chuckled. 'What else?'

'She was beautiful. And *fun*. And she loved kids. She wanted a dozen. I think she would have too, you know,' she said, shifting to look up at him, her eyes misting. 'She'd have made a great mother.'

Gareth's heart swelled in his chest. 'It sucks.'

'Yes. It does.'

'It helps to talk, though.'

She nodded. 'Yes. It does. And sometimes…' her gaze zeroed in on his mouth and it tingled so hard it hurt '…it helps not to talk at all.'

Gareth sucked in a breath. He couldn't agree more.

CHAPTER SIXTEEN

BILLIE WHIMPERED WHEN Gareth's mouth took hers in an achingly tender kiss. It was sweet and soft, warm and gentle, exploring the contours of her mouth in unhurried detail.

It broke her and healed her all at once.

When he pulled away, Billie's head was swimming from its intensity. 'No,' she murmured, reaching for him. Needing him to do it again.

'Shh,' he whispered against her mouth, as he dropped another gentle kiss on her lips. 'Not here,' he said, extricating himself and standing, holding his hand out to her. 'I want to lay you out on my bed. I want to look at you.'

Billie's stomach dropped right out as his words washed over her. She slid her hand into his and stood, her legs trembling in anticipation. Gareth smiled at her and led her though the house, down a darkened hallway, until they reached the double doors at the end.

He pushed one open and tugged her in after him.

The low-lit room was beautiful but Billie didn't notice the expensive furnishings or the plush carpet underfoot, she only had eyes for Gareth, who was turning and taking her in his arms again, kissing her mouth and her eyes and her nose. Nuzzling her ear and her neck, his hands stroking down her back, pushing underneath her jumper and her top to find her bare flesh.

'Off,' he muttered in her ear, pushing both pieces of clothing up. 'I want to kiss you all over.'

Billie didn't have to be asked twice as she ducked her head out of the clothing and Gareth flung them on the floor.

His breath hissed out as she stood before him in her bra and track pants. His gaze devoured her and her nipples beaded before his thorough inspection. He traced a finger from the hollow of her throat to the cleavage of her bra.

'I knew you'd be this beautiful,' he whispered, his eyes never leaving her, his fingers stroking lightly along her collarbones. 'I haven't been able to stop thinking about you.'

Billie's eyes fluttered closed under his silky caress.

'I've dreamed about being inside you,' he said, and her eyes opened at his frank admission. He sank on his knees before her and kissed her belly. She sank her hand into his crinkly hair as his tongue dipped into her navel.

'Gareth,' she moaned, her legs threatening to give away.

He grabbed her other hand and placed it on his shoulder and Billie held on for dear life, bunching his shirt in her hands as his tongue traced from one hip to the other.

'Damn...you taste good.' She felt his groan hot against her belly.

Billie whimpered at the want and ache in his voice. Ached for him too. Wanted to touch him, put her mouth to him as he was to her. She grabbed at his shirt, hauled it up, yanking him up with it, whipping it off, her greedy hands going to his chest, feeling the heat, her palms revelling in the rough smatter of hair as he plundered her mouth, squeezing her buttocks, urging her closer.

And then his palms were sliding beneath the waistband of her track pants, sizzling against the bare flesh of her bottom, and she moaned against his mouth as his thumbs hooked into the band sitting on her hips and pulled it down, her underwear going too. He eased them over her hips, his palms pushing them down her legs.

Billie kicked out of them and then she was completely naked, conscious of the erotic scrape of denim against the bare skin of her thighs and the smooth play of his hands as they caressed her buttocks, kneading and stroking, urging her closer to him.

'Bed,' he said, pulling away slightly to walk her closer to the mattress, stopping when the backs of her thighs hit the edge, urging her to sit, to lie back.

She sat. She lay.

She stretched her arms above her head and looked right at him.

'God…Billie…' he said, his breath rough, 'the things I want to do to you.'

Billie smiled, her nipples peaking under his hot gaze. She lifted her leg and hooked it around the back of his thighs. 'Bit hard to do it from all the way up there,' she murmured.

He slid a hand onto her thigh. 'I just want to look at you some more.'

Billie's cheeks warmed as he did exactly that. Pinned to the bed by the raw sexuality in his blue gaze, her neck flushed, her nipples ruched into tight, hard pebbles, her belly tightened.

The tingling at the juncture of her thighs went from buzz to burn.

'Gareth,' she complained, her voice almost a pant. She was going to die from the anticipation if he didn't do something. 'You promised me Elvis.'

His hand tightened on her thigh and he grinned. 'Do you see me talking?'

'You're talking with your eyes.'

He laughed then. 'Damn straight. Do you know what they're saying?'

'No.' She grimaced. 'But I'm guessing you're going to tell me.'

He grinned again. 'They're saying…where do I start first? Do I stroke? Do I kiss? Do I lick?'

Billie bit back a full-blown moan. 'I'm good with any combination.'

'Do I start at your mouth and work down?' he mused, following that path with his eyes. 'Or do I start at your toes and head up? Or do I just zero in on one bit. And, if so, which bit? Your neck?' His gaze dropped to her breasts, 'Your nipples?' It lingered there for long moments and Billie suppressed the urge to arch her back. 'Or do I start a little further south?'

His gaze moved down to the juncture of her thighs and Billie swallowed—hard.

'You're like a smorgasbord,' he murmured, staring at her there. 'And I'm really, really hungry.'

Billie's leg clamped hard around his thigh. 'Damn it, Gareth,' she groaned. 'A little less conversation.'

He chuckled, cranking her frustration up another notch. 'Where do you want me first?'

'Just kiss me,' she half moaned, half begged, reaching for him. 'Kiss me anywhere.'

And then he crawled on the bed over top of her and kissed her. Long and deep and so exquisitely Billie wanted to cry for the beauty of it. It sucked away her breath and twenty-six years of being an Ashworth-Keyes as she linked her arms around his neck and fell headlong into the perfect insanity.

They kissed for an age. Universes were born and died and still he kissed her. Taking his time, savouring her taste and her moans and sighs. Billie let him lead, followed him eagerly as her own hands explored the contours of his neck, his shoulders, his back. Her fingers brushed the denim waistband of his jeans and pushed beneath, finding other contours, better contours to squeeze and knead.

Suddenly, impatient with any barrier between them, her fingers came around to the front, delving between their bodies, nudging open his button and his zip and pushing at the fabric, taking his underwear as well, easing them both down over his hips as he had done to her.

He lifted, shifted to give her access, wriggled and kicked

out of the denim, not breaking his lip lock once, and then he was naked, settling between her thighs, taunting her mercilessly with a slow rub, the long, hard length of him easing through all her slick heat.

'God…you feel so good. So wet…' he groaned against her mouth. 'I want to be inside you.'

'*Gareth*,' Billie gasped, at the strained urgency of his words and the slow erotic grind. She dug her nails into his back. 'Yes,' she panted. 'God…please…yes.'

He lifted away from her and Billie was momentarily bereft. 'No,' she protested, grabbing for him.

He came back to her, kissed her. 'It's okay,' he murmured, dropping soothing kisses against her mouth, her nose, her eyelids. 'Just getting a condom.'

And then he was gone again but he was back quickly and sheathing himself and settling between her legs again and she was opening wide to him, lifting her hips, locking her legs around his waist, blatantly inviting him inside.

She gasped at the first thick nudge of him and when he entered her completely, sliding all the way in, she arched her back and cried out.

'Billie,' he panted, burying his face in her neck.

Billie slid her hands onto his buttocks, clenching them hard in her hands, holding him tight, right where he was as he pressed and stretched all the right spots. 'Feels so good,' she muttered.

He chuckled into her neck and it was sweet and sexy all at once, fanning hot breath onto her sensitised skin. Then he planted the flats of his arms on either side of her head and lifted himself up, rearing over her, their chests apart, their hips joined, his eyes looking right down into hers.

'Hold on,' he said. 'It's going to feel better.'

He moved then, flexing his hips, and she gasped again, gripping his back as he pulled out and slid back in, thick and sure. Billie shut her eyes as pleasure shimmied through the nerve fibres in her belly and thighs.

He was right, it felt *so* much better.

'Look at me.'

Billie opened her eyes and saw his blue gaze piercing her. 'I want to watch you come,' he said, pulling out. 'I want you to be...' he eased into her oh-so-slowly '...looking right at me.'

Billie nodded but her eyes closed involuntarily as his hardness stretched every last millimetre of her and everything clenched inside.

'Billie.' They snapped open at the raw command. 'I said...' he pulled out '...open.' He pushed in.

Billie fought the urge to close them again as pleasure pulled at her eyelids. She groaned, gripped his buttocks, as the maddeningly slow pace continued. 'Come on, Gareth, faster.'

'No.' He grimaced, the veins in his neck standing out. 'I'm going to make you come so slowly you're going to feel every...' he eased in '...single...' he eased out '...second.'

He eased all the way in again.

And it was working. A flutter pulsed low in her belly as she gripped the hard length of him.

'You're beautiful,' he murmured, looking down at her, burying his fingers in her hair as he kept up the slow and easy pace. 'I've wanted you since that first night, at the accident. I could hardly take my eyes off you.'

'Oh, yeah?' she panted. 'Was that before or after I tossed my cookies?' He hit a sweet spot and she gasped, anchoring her hands to his shoulders and flexing her hips. 'Oh, God, yes, just there,' she said, all high and breathy.

He obliged, angling himself just right, massaging the spot back and forth with the same steady thrusts, cranking up the flutter.

'God, Billie,' he groaned, as he thrust and held tight, seating himself deep. 'You make me crazy. I can't believe I kissed you in the tearoom...I so should not have done that.'

'Yes,' she moaned, as she flexed her hips some more, encouraging him to go deeper. 'You should have.' She looked into his eyes. 'I wanted it.' She locked her legs around his waist, lifting her hips again. 'I *needed* it.'

It was satisfying to see his eyes shut, hear the hiss of his breath. 'Damn it, Billie,' he groaned, his eyes flashing open, piercing her with hungry eyes as he clamped a hand to her hip. 'Stop wriggling like that.'

Billie shook her head, circling her hips again, daring him with her gaze. 'You've kept me waiting for weeks, Gareth.' She clenched internal muscles around him. 'Enough already.'

Gareth groaned then dropped his head, kissing her hard, surging inside her as he released her hip, his elbows digging into the bed either side of her head, giving him greater purchase. 'I wanted to go inside with you that morning in the car,' he said, pulling away from her mouth, his own moist from their passion. He rocked into her. 'And that night, at your place…'

Billie could see his biceps flexing in her peripheral vision as he slid in and out. 'You're here now,' she said, lifting her head, nuzzling his lips. 'So do me already.'

And she kissed him, hot and hard, putting every ounce of herself into it. Showing him the extent of her need, the depths of her desperation. Whimpering, 'Please,' against his mouth. Laying herself bare. Making herself vulnerable to him in a way she'd never done with another man. Needing his possession as much as she needed oxygen.

Did he want her to beg? Because she'd do that too.

Billie was breathing hard when she pulled out of the kiss. So was he.

Gareth looked down at her, his gaze roving over her face, her neck, her breasts, his chest heaving. 'Like this?' he asked, pumping his hips a little quicker.

Billie moaned as he hit all the right spots. 'God…yes.' Her head dropped back, her belly tightened.

He sped up some more. 'You want it like this?' he demanded.

Billie whimpered. 'Yes,' she gasped. 'More.'

'Like this?' he panted, his gaze snagging hers as his thrusts steadily picked up tempo, rocking her head, driving her higher and higher.

The flutter turned into a ripple.

She grabbed his buttocks. 'Yes.'

'You want it hard and fast?' he demanded.

Billie moaned, finding his blue gaze utterly compelling. 'God, yes.' Meaty muscles flexed in her hands with each thrust and she held them fast, anchored herself there.

'More?'

'Yes.' Her heart thundered, her breath rasped. The ripple became a contraction. 'Don't stop,' she gasped. 'Don't. Ever. Stop.'

He didn't. He drove into her relentlessly, their bodies meshed as one, their gazes locked. The contractions multiplied, rippling out, her consciousness slowly fraying at the edges. 'Yes, yes,' she sobbed, her eyes widening, as a wave of pleasure washed over her.

'Yes,' he muttered triumphantly, as she tightened around him. 'That's it…yes. Hold on, I've got you.'

And then as more waves broke he slowed it right down. Billie whimpered as he pulsed in and out slowly, rocking her gently, sweetly, wringing every ounce of pleasure out of each contraction, prolonging it to an unbearable intensity.

She shut her eyes. It was too much. It was going to kill her. She was going to die, die here in his arms, gasping in pleasure. 'Look at me, damn it, Billie,' he demanded.

She looked at him as she slowly came apart.

'Look at what you do to me.'

He groaned then, long and low, his blue gaze heating to flame, his arms trembling, his hips thrusting hard, jerking to a standstill as he cried out.

Billie gripped him hard, his pleasure feeding hers, the honesty in his eyes overwhelming. 'Yes,' she whispered, snaking a hand up into his hair, twisting her fingers hard into his wavy locks, dragging his head down. 'More,' she said against his lips.

'Yes,' he said, kissing her, moving his hips again.

Billie moaned into his mouth as the pulsing continued unabated, her entire body buffeted by waves of intense pleasure. 'Good,' she whispered. 'So good.'

'Yes,' he agreed.

And he kissed her all the way to the end. Until he collapsed on top of her and they were both gasping and sated.

CHAPTER SEVENTEEN

GARETH WOKE A few hours later with Billie spooning him, her hand lightly stroking his hip. His groin was already well and truly awake. He smiled. 'A little lower.'

Billie laughed as his low rumble vibrated along muscle fibres already in a state of excitability. She slid her hand onto his solid thigh and then down onto his erection.

'Lower?'

Gareth grunted, shutting his eyes as she slid her hand up and down. 'No,' he said, shunting in a ragged breath. 'That's just right.'

She played a little longer before sliding her hand up to his shoulder and urging him onto his back. She threw her leg across his body and claimed his lips and then, before she knew it, he was pulling her over on top of him, settling the slick juncture of her thighs against the hot, hard length of him.

She rubbed herself against his delicious thickness, pleasure pouring heat into the cauldron of her pelvis.

'Mmm,' he murmured, stroking her back. 'That feels good.'

Billie sighed, stilling against him, enjoying the feel of his girth, hard and good, pressing into all her softness. She rested her cheek on his pec, the thud of Gareth's heart and the slow, lazy patterns he was stroking over her back lulling her eyes shut.

Gareth shut his eyes too, remembering how nice this part was. Lying with a woman afterwards. Touching her. Snuggling in the glow. Every nerve ending sated and energised at the same time. Feeling lazy and heavy but also light and floaty.

He opened his eyes after a while. Billie's breathing was deep and even and he wondered if she was asleep. 'Thank you,' he said into the dark. 'I've missed this.'

Billie stirred from the trancelike state she'd entered. She lifted her head to look at him. 'Am I your first…I mean, since Catherine…? Has there been anyone else?'

He smiled at her, his hand stroking down the side of her face, tucking a strand of hair behind her ear. 'Why? Was I that rusty?'

Billie laughed as she made two fists on his chest and propped her chin on them. 'If that was you rusty I hope I'm around for when you're well oiled.'

He grinned at her and Billie's heart hitched a little. 'If we keep going this way, that should be by morning.'

She smiled. 'Lucky me.'

Gareth picked up another lock of her hair and sifted it through his fingers. Lying in the dark with her, her body warm and supple, her breasts pressed against his chest, he felt like he could tell her anything.

'I've had a couple of brief liaisons since Catherine died. One was at a conference. A one-night stand thing. The other was a mother from Amber's school, who'd just been through a rough divorce and was after a little revenge sex.'

Billie smiled, despite the spike of jealousy niggling at her chest. 'She chose well.'

He chuckled. 'It was good. Fun. The first time was only a couple of months after Catherine had died. I was…lost, I guess.' He sought her gaze as he rubbed a copper lock between his finger pads. 'I missed her so much. I wanted to stop feeling so awful, to forget for a while. But…I felt even more awful after, like I'd cheated on her. The second time,

AMY ANDREWS 141

Laura, was much later. I was more emotionally ready for it. And I…needed it. I needed to feel like a man again, a fully functioning man.'

Billie sobered. She understood what he was telling her. It was only natural for a man who had lost the love of his life to go through the entire gamut of emotional responses to that loss.

But it beggared the question—what was she? Was she just another signpost on his journey through grief?

She absently traced her finger around his nipple, the hairs tickling. 'Is that was this is? Am I helping you feel like a man again?'

Gareth frowned. Her tone was light but her eyes had gone all serious. 'What? No.' He grabbed her hand. He couldn't concentrate when she was touching him like that. 'No,' he reiterated, bringing her fingers to his mouth and kissing them.

He shifted then, taking her with him as he rolled over, rolling her under him, his body half on, half off her, his thigh parting her legs, pinning them to the bed. He propped himself up on an elbow.

He needed her to understand what she meant. What their coming together tonight meant to him.

Gareth pushed his hand into her hair and stroked his thumb along her cheekbone as he looked into her eyes.

'You're the first woman since my wife died that's meant *anything* to me. For the first time in five years this isn't about me or my grief or what I want or need. I'm attracted to you, because of *you.* And I know the way you know things deep down in your gut that this can't possibly last but I really *like* you, Billie.'

'Yes.' She smiled. 'You told me already.'

'No.' This wasn't the same thing as their fake-date thing. 'I *like you* like you.'

Billie's heart squeezed in her chest at his sudden seriousness. It wasn't the L word that most women her age seemed to long for but it was such an earnest, heartfelt sentiment that

Billie drank it up. Gareth had been through so much, lost so much. That he was even capable of feeling anything again was a miracle. And she cherished it.

She smiled at him. 'I *like* you too.'

'It's okay, I don't expect a reciprocal admission. That wasn't why I said it. I just know I feel very deeply for you already. And I wanted you know it too. I wanted you to know that you're not some way for me to prove that I still have all my working bits or that you're some diversion to keep the blackness at bay. You're not *just* my two-yearly roll in the hay.'

He kissed her then, slow and gentle. Kissed her until she moaned and clung and begged him for more.

They finally woke around nine. Slow and easy at first as they drifted up through layers of sleep then hot and heavy as their bodies woke and desire, sweet and heady, surged through their systems.

'I think I could get used to this,' he murmured.

Billie sighed. She could definitely get used to waking up with Gareth. It would be *no* hardship. She snuggled into him. 'Me too.'

Gareth's hands found her breasts and his groin perked up again. He was surprised it was still physically able after last night. He was about to suggest going again when a loud growl emanated from her stomach. Gareth laughed.

'Wow. That's a helluva belly rumble. I'm impressed.'

Billie blushed at her noisy innards. 'Sorry.' She slid her hand over her navel. 'It must be all that physical activity you put me through. I'm starving.'

'Put you through.' He chuckled again. 'Didn't seem like a chore when you were screaming my name all night,' he murmured, nipping at the patch of skin where shoulder met neck. She sucked in a breath and her nipples beaded in his palm. 'I make some mean French toast. Or would you prefer jam on toast?'

Billie smiled as her stomach rumbled again. 'I *love* French toast. Do you have banana?'

'Yes. And bacon. And maple syrup'

'You are a god amongst men.'

He grinned. 'Damn straight.' He kissed her neck then extricated himself, dropping his head down to kiss her hip before leaving the bed. He grabbed his underwear off the floor and climbed into it before turning to look at her. She'd rolled onto her back, not bothering to pull the sheet up. His gaze wandered up and down the length of her and his recipe for French toast slipped away.

Her stomach growled again and he shook his head. 'Why don't you come and keep me company?'

Billie arched an eyebrow. 'Like this?'

He nodded. 'Exactly like that. You could be my muse while I create food for you. Of course, I couldn't promise that you won't end up covered in maple syrup.'

Billie's head filled with a very erotic image of her spread out on the kitchen bench while he licked maple syrup out of her belly button. And other places. Thinking about where she could lick it off him was equally erotic.

She rolled up onto her elbow and she liked the way his gaze wandered to the fall of her breasts. 'Let me take a shower first. Maybe bring it back to bed after?'

Gareth liked the way she thought. He particularly liked the way she thought when she was naked in his bed. 'Good thinking.' His gaze drifted down to where the sheet cut across low on her hips, hiding one of her best bits from his view.

A fine spot for maple syrup if ever there was one.

Billie was pretty sure she knew where his mind was and her toes curled beneath the sheet. 'You could always, of course, join me?' she suggested, slowly trailing her palm down the middle of her belly, bringing it to a halt where sheet met skin. His gaze snagged on the movement and she smiled as she slid her fingers under the edge slightly. 'You could make sure I get all those *nooks and crannies* clean?'

Gareth dragged in a shaky breath. He wanted to rip that sheet back and dive between her legs. Make her come so loud she'd be sure to think twice about teasing him so blatantly.

For sure he wanted to take her against the tiles of his shower.

He dragged his gaze to her face. 'Do you want to eat at some stage today? Because if I get you in the shower all wet and slippery, there's no way I'm letting you out for a *very long time.*'

Billie smiled as he snatched up his jeans and left without a backward glance.

She sighed. The man really did have a spectacular butt.

CHAPTER EIGHTEEN

GARETH HAD CLIMBED into his jeans and was whistling by the time he hit the kitchen. He shouldn't be. He had a hunch, despite them both admitting to having feelings for each other, that things with Billie weren't going to run smoothly. She was pretty messed up about her life direction and grief had made him wary, more cautious with his heart.

But today he didn't much care about any of that.

He flicked the radio on. Rock music blared out loud and perfect and he bopped his head to the exhilarating beat as he clanged around in the kitchen, barefoot, bare-chested and one hundred per cent lord of all he surveyed.

He felt indomitable. He felt like a freaking king.

He felt like throwing his head back and crying out Tarzan-style as he beat his chest.

Gareth, King of the Jungle!

He smiled at the notion as he cracked the eggs into a bowl. He couldn't remember the last time he'd felt this good. He certainly hadn't felt this deep down happy with either of his last two liaisons.

Sure, Laura had been fun, a brief superficial distraction that he'd enjoyed very much, but she hadn't left him feeling this bone-deep satisfaction.

This feeling that all was right with the world.

Maybe he was getting ahead of himself. Maybe hormones and endorphins were making him delirious.

But nothing could erase his happy this morning.

* * *

Billie towelled off and headed back into the bedroom for her clothes. They lay scattered around the floor and her stomach dropped just remembering everything that had happened since she'd shed those suckers last night.

She picked them up, figuring she could get back into her track pants and turtleneck. She didn't want to get back into her undies but she could go without. If she played her cards right they'd be back in bed before too much longer anyway.

She smiled as she plotted how she might drop her commando state into their breakfast conversation. Or was that brunch?

She quickly jammed a foot into the leg of her track pants, her gaze taking in her surroundings properly for the first time as she stuck her other foot in and pulled the track pants up. The dishevelled bed dominated the room. Off one wall was the en suite. Off the other a walk-in wardrobe.

Billie grinned to herself. Oh, the possibilities!

She sauntered over. Maybe she could find something clean of Gareth's to get into instead?

The wardrobe was extensive but most of it was empty except for a small section of hanging clothes and some occupied drawers. She figured the owners must have taken all their clothes with them and what was left was Gareth's.

She riffled through his hanging clothes and found a russet-coloured business shirt that matched her hair perfectly. She inhaled the sunshine and soap-powder smell of it before removing it from the hanger and shoving her arms through the sleeves.

She turned and inspected herself in the full-length mirror. Her hair was still knotted on top of her head and she quickly released it, shaking it out, watching as it fell down around her shoulders.

She stripped off her track pants and she liked what she saw—pink cheeks, glowing skin, sparkling eyes. She didn't look tired as she probably should be, considering how little sleep she'd had. On the contrary, she looked like a woman who had been kept up all night in the best possible way.

She looked thoroughly sated.

On impulse, Billie undid the top two and bottom two buttons, leaving only two in the middle holding the shirt together. An enticing slice of bare breasts and a glimpse of shadow at the juncture of her thighs looked back at her.

She put her hand on her hip and pouted at her reflection. The action drew the hem of the shirt up even higher, revealing a much bigger glimpse of what was below her navel.

Not the effect she was going for.

She turned to his drawers and searched for some underwear, smiling when she found a pair of fluro green boxers. *Perfect.*

She slipped them on. They were on the baggy side but she rolled the waistband low on her hips and it anchored there well enough. She went back to the mirror, giving herself a once-over. A barely recognisable woman stared back at her. With her hair all loose, her mouth all pouty and cleavage to burn, she looked far from a responsible emergency medicine doctor.

She certainly didn't look like an Ashworth-Keyes.

No. She looked like one of those old-fashioned sex kittens from the magazines of the forties and fifties.

Billie smiled. She hoped Gareth *liked* it too.

Gareth was so engrossed in the music, juggling the cooking of the French toast and the bacon and thinking about how good Billie would look all wet and naked in the shower, he didn't hear the key in the lock or the door open.

He was well and truly in his happy place.

So much so he actually startled when Amber appeared in front of him, saying, 'God, that smell's amazing. Remind me to flip out more often, would you?'

He blinked at his daughter uncomprehendingly for a few moments. 'Amber?'

She laughed. 'Correct. Are you okay? You're looking weird.' She stepped forward and kissed him on the cheek, swiping a piece of piping-hot, crispy bacon off the plate.

Gareth couldn't think for a moment. Crap!

Amber.

She'd been to that support group yesterday and he'd forgotten he'd invited her for breakfast this morning!

'Ooh, French toast?' she murmured, oblivious to his turmoil. 'You've outdone yourself. Great timing too. It's as if you knew I was about to walk through the door.'

He smiled as he gathered his scattered wits. He needed to talk and fast. Billie was bound to be showing her face any time soon. 'Yes. About that…'

Billie followed the sound of music and the smell of frying bacon all the way to the kitchen. Her mouth watered and her stomach rumbled louder.

'Hope you've made double,' she announced as she entered the kitchen. 'You wore me out last night, I need sus—'

Billie stopped abruptly when she realised Gareth wasn't alone in the kitchen.

Amber?

'Oh.' She looked from Gareth to a shocked Amber then back to Gareth again. 'I'm sorry. I didn't realise you had… company…'

Billie wished the floor would open up and swallow her in the tense silence that followed. Suddenly her forties sex-kitten look seemed cheap and tawdry. Or at least that must be how it looked to Gareth's daughter.

Amber looked at her father. 'Who the hell is *she*?'

Gareth grimaced at the poison in Amber's words. She was looking at him with eyes full of anger and confusion and he'd give anything to rewind the last couple of minutes.

He and Amber had never talked about what would happen when this day swung around. When he became involved with another woman.

He'd always figured when—*if*—it did, that it would be a gradual thing and Amber would be along for the ride.

He hadn't expected to be sprung fresh out of bed by his twenty-year-old daughter.

He held up both his hands. Amber looked like she was going to bolt and he didn't want her leaving without knowing that this wasn't what she was thinking. 'I'm sorry, Amber. I forgot you were coming over this morning.'

Clearly the wrong thing to say as Amber went from frosty anger to visible hurt. But she recovered quickly, her wounded eyes turning as hard as stone. 'I just bet you did,' she snapped, whirling away.

'Amber...' he said, striding across the room to stop her exit. He grabbed her arm. 'Let me explain.'

'What are you going to tell me?' she demanded, whirling back to face him. 'That this isn't what I think it is? That this... woman isn't wearing the shirt I bought you for Christmas last year and you haven't been *screwing h*er all night long?'

Billie's audible gasp sliced through him. 'Amber, that's enough.' This had obviously come as a shock to her and it certainly wasn't the way he'd have hoped Amber found out about his private life but he wouldn't let her cheapen what had happened between him and Billie either.

Amber glared at him. 'Screw you too,' she said, jerking her arm out of his grasp and storming out of the house.

Fabulous. Beautifully handled.

Not.

He turned back to Billie, his brain churning with a hundred different things to say, none of them particularly adequate in the face of her stillness or pallor. She was standing, apparently frozen to the spot in the middle of the kitchen, every cute freckle dusting the bridge of her nose standing out.

The fact that she looked so incredibly sexy in his shirt was a particular irony. Amber's impromptu arrival had blown any chance of him getting her out of it now.

He raked a hand through his hair. 'Sorry about that.'

His words prodded Billie out of her inertia. She shook her head. 'It's fine.'

'I…forgot.' He rubbed his eyes. 'I forgot I invited her over.'

Billie nodded. She didn't think Gareth had deliberately set this up for some fairy-tale meet-cute. If he had, it had seriously backfired.

'It's fine,' she said again.

'She's just found out that she has the BRCA1 gene,' he said. 'She went to some support group yesterday. We were supposed to be debriefing this morning but—'

But.

Billie didn't need him to fill in the blanks. She was the *but*. It was *her* fault he'd forgotten. S*he'd* distracted him from his parental responsibilities.

'I'm sorry to hear that,' she said, hugging herself as she sucked in a breath around the painful lump in the centre of her chest. It was stupid to feel slighted—this wasn't about her. Amber must be reeling from the dreadful news. 'She must be feeling very vulnerable at the moment.'

If she kept this about Amber, Billie knew she could keep everything in perspective. And it should be about Amber. The twenty-year-old had just been dealt a huge whammy. It was nothing compared to whatever fledgling thing they had going on.

He rubbed the back of his neck. 'It's been a shock.'

Billie nodded. Of course it had. She only had to look at Gareth's face to know how much it was eating him up. 'I'm just…going to go,' she said.

Gareth looked at her in alarm. 'No…Billie…' He joined her in the kitchen in four easy strides, sliding his hands onto her waist.

He knew he'd gaffed with her too. This morning when

he'd woken up he'd felt bulletproof. And then Amber had thrown one hell of a spanner in the works.

'I didn't mean to imply that this Amber thing is your fault. *I* messed this up.'

Billie held up her hand. 'It's fine. *I'm* fine. You should go to her. You need to talk to Amber.'

And she needed some time and space. Billie was still struggling to assimilate what had happened. She guessed it was inevitable that reality would intrude into their bubble sooner or later but she'd figured she'd have a little more time. And reality would come in the form of work or her family, not in the form of Gareth's rightfully furious daughter.

The reality of Gareth's life was that he was a forty-year-old father and that had to be the main priority in his life. The reality was that they *both* had other priorities in their life—how could it ever work?

Reality was a bitch like that.

Gareth sighed. He knew she was right. He had to go after Amber but he didn't want to leave it like this with Billie either. 'Can I see you tonight?'

She stepped out of his arms. 'I'm having dinner with my family tonight.'

It was the first time Billie had ever been grateful for one of the tediously long, pompous do's she was subjected to every month.

'I'll see you at work on Monday, though, right?' she added.

Gareth may have been off the market for a long time but he knew a brush-off when he saw it. Although, to be fair to Billie, this had to be a little overwhelming.

Maybe it was good to have some space.

'Sure,' he said.

'Okay… I'll just…' she looked over her shoulder '…grab my stuff, then.'

Gareth watched her go, thoughts churning around his head as he absently dealt with the half-cooked breakfast. She was back in the kitchen in under five minutes, wearing her clothes from last night. The brief goodbye peck on the cheek she gave him was not encouraging.

Neither was the way she didn't look back as she strode out of his house.

CHAPTER NINETEEN

GARETH WAS STANDING on Amber's doorstep an hour later. He'd showered and changed first, knowing from old that giving Amber some time to cool down always boded well.

Carly answered the door. 'You're in the doghouse,' she said in her usual blunt manner.

'Yes.' Gareth grimaced. 'Can I come in?'

'I think her exact words were, "If that rat shows up here, kick his butt to the kerb."'

Gareth ignored the insult, quirking an eyebrow. 'Is that what you're here to do?'

Carly was possibly the most petite female he knew. Sure, she made up for it with her big, ballsy personality but he could have pushed her aside with one finger.

Carly opened the door wider and stepped aside. 'Nope. She needs to talk to you. She just doesn't know it yet.'

He grinned. 'I've always liked you.'

'Got your back, Jack,' Carly quipped, as Gareth entered.

'So…how is she…really?' he asked, after Carly shut the door.

Carly shrugged. 'I think she's on her bed, sticking pins in an effigy of you.'

Gareth chuckled but quickly sobered. 'I messed up, Carly.'

'Yeah.' Carly nodded. 'She said. But you know what I told her?'

'No, what?'

'That any other hottie father who'd been through what you'd been through would probably have blown through a stack of sympathetic chicks by now and it was about time she stopped putting you on some exalted pedestal and realised you're just flesh and blood. And that Catherine wouldn't have wanted you to be alone for ever.'

Even as an eight-year-old, Carly had said stuff that had been designed to shock, so he ignored her *hottie father* reference. But she'd always been a wise little thing. 'Oh.'

'Yeah...I think she's sticking pins in an effigy of me too.'

Gareth chuckled. 'Well, thank you. That can't have been easy.'

Carly shrugged. 'Ya gotta know when to hand out the tissues and when to dish out some tough love. Breast cancer gene gets tissues. Daddy's got a girlfriend after being a widower for five long lonely years not so much.'

Gareth was grateful that Amber had such a good friend in Carly. He knew Catherine's death had devastated Carly too. He glanced down the hall at Amber's door.

'Going in, then. Wish me luck.'

'You won't need it,' Carly said, shaking her head. 'She can never stay mad at you for long.'

Gareth snorted. 'She was angry at me for two years.'

'That's different. Her mother had died. You think anything's worse than that?'

Gareth shook his head. 'Good point.'

Gareth knocked on the door but didn't wait for permission to enter. It was unlocked so he pushed it open.

'Go away,' Amber said, glaring at him from the bed. Her eyes were red-rimmed and puffy-looking but there were no effigies in sight.

'I think we should talk.'

'I don't want to talk to you.'

'Fine... I'll talk and you can listen.'

Amber stared at him mutinously, crossing her arms. 'How about you turn around and don't come back?'

Gareth shook his head, not easily deterred. 'I'm really sorry about earlier. You coming over had slipped my mind and—'

Amber's snort interrupted him. 'I wonder why?'

'Yes,' Gareth sighed. 'Billie being there distracted me.'

'Billie? That's a stupid name.'

Gareth would have laughed at the childish comeback had he not already been walking a delicate line. 'It's actually Willamina. Willamina Ashworth-Keyes. She's one of the new residents at work.'

'You think I should be impressed that you can pull a doctor?' she said scornfully.

'No, of course not…' Gareth sighed, risking sitting on the edge of Amber's bed. 'I just thought you might like to know more about her.'

'Why?' she flared back at him. 'Is she going to be my new mummy?'

Gareth took a breath and searched for the deeper meaning to the scathing question, like the hospital counsellors had urged him to do. 'You're angry because you think I'm replacing Catherine? That I'm forgetting her?'

'No,' Amber denied hotly, but Gareth could see the hurt in her eyes. 'I'm angry because we were supposed to spend the morning together but you *forgot* because you were too busy with your new girlfriend.'

'She's not my girlfriend, Amber. We've just met. It's just new…' He looked down at his hands as he remembered Billie's noncommittal departure. 'I'm not even certain it's going anywhere.'

'But you're in love with her.'

He glanced at Amber sharply. Her puffy eyes looked deadly serious and they were demanding the truth. 'We *just* met,' he repeated.

Amber shook her head at him, her lip curling. 'How *old* is she?'

'She's twenty-six.'

'Bloody hell, Gareth!'

'Yes.' The thought was depressing. 'That is one of the complications.'

'Didn't stop you sleeping with her, though, did it?'

'Amber,' he warned. 'I'm not going to talk about my sex life with you.'

'Oh…so you have a *sex life* now?' she demanded.

Gareth grimaced. 'Probably not after today, no…'

Amber didn't say anything for a long time, she just looked at him, her gaze roving over his face, searching for what, he didn't know. But slowly the anger drained from her face.

'You do love her.'

Gareth shook his head. He wished he knew how he felt. 'I don't know, Amba-san. I know I like her. I like her a lot. But it's complicated. She's at a different stage in her life to me.'

Another snort but this one was softer, more mocking than angry. 'No kidding.'

He gave a half-laugh, relieved that Amber's anger had dissipated. He could still see shadows in her gaze but she'd had them since she'd been fifteen.

Amber swung her legs over the side of the bed. 'I'm sorry. I didn't mean to flip out the way I did. I guess I'm doing that quite a bit lately,' she said quietly.

He shrugged. 'You're dealing with a lot.'

'I was…shocked. I guess part of me always thought you'd be faithful to Mum for ever. I know that's not fair to you, though. Carly says I need to cut you some slack and that you're just flesh and blood.'

Gareth smiled. He leaned in closer to her and nudged her arm with his. 'I think we should keep Carly.'

'As if we could get rid of her.'

They laughed then and it felt good after the emotionally charged morning. When they stopped Gareth looked down at his daughter. 'I'm always going to love your mum, Amba-san. No matter what my future holds, she'll always be…' he tapped his chest '…here.'

She turned her face to him and tears were swimming in her big eyes, so like her mother's. 'I have this dream every now and then… I can't remember what she looks like. What if I forget what she looks like, Gareth?'

Gareth put his arm around her shoulder and hugged her to his side. 'You won't forget. Her image is engraved on your heart. And, anyway, there are too many pictures of her around.'

'Don't you ever worry you will?'

Gareth shook his head. 'No. She's engraved on my heart too. And even if for some obscure reason I did and every single picture of the thousands we have were destroyed, I'd just need to look at you.'

They sat together for long moments. He kissed her on the head again. 'You okay now?'

Amber nodded, looking up at him. 'I guess we'd better go and let Carly know she's not going to need to bury a body.'

'Comforting to know she would, though,' Gareth said, smiling as he took Amber's hand and they stood together and headed for the door.

At nine-thirty Billie was ready to fake a heart attack to get away early from the family dinner. But dessert was yet to be served and an Ashworth-Keyes did not leave before dessert, coffee, liqueurs and every single grotesque medical story since the last time they had met had been told.

And it *was* only once a month.

In between grilling her about the emergency department at St Luke's, her grandfather, her parents, two uncles and three cousins were discussing a surgical case that had hit the news due to mismanagement. If she heard the words 'faecal peritonitis' one more time she was going to throw up her beef Wellington.

Did they really have to talk about such things while they were *eating?*

Of course, she should be used to it now—she'd grown up with medical chitchat forming the basis of most teatime conversation, but it all seemed so...clinical. Billie had an insane urge to mention Jessica—something they never talked about—just to get a human, non-medical reaction.

She didn't. *Of course.*

That would be very un-Ashworth-Keyes of her.

But her mind kept drifting to where she'd been this time last night, preferring the memory of being naked with Gareth than anything going on at the table. And when it wasn't there, it was reliving the nightmare of Amber's 'Who the hell is *she*?'

Coming face to face with the reality of Gareth's life had been a wake-up call. She hadn't handled it very well. But running away from things was what she did best.

'Billie?'

Billie blinked as her father's harsh voice dragged her out of the events of this morning. All eyes were on her. 'I'm sorry?'

He sighed impatiently. 'What on earth is the matter with you tonight? Why are you so distracted?' he demanded.

The whole table was looking at her, apparently waiting for her response. 'I'm just...tired,' she said lamely, dismissing her father's query with a wave of her hand.

'*Tired!*' her father snorted, as if it was something only lazy people suffered. If only he knew how very little sleep she'd had last night. 'A good doctor pushes through that barrier.'

And then he went off on a tangent about his days of training and how many hours they'd worked and how little time off they'd had, and then her grandfather and uncles joined in and Billie let her mind drift again.

Her phone vibrated in her pocket and she leapt for it as

if it was a lifeline and she was drowning. Her father glared at her as she checked the text message. She didn't care. She knew it was bad table manners but so was talking about gruesome surgeries, as far as she was concerned.

Sorry about this morning. Things better with Amber. Thinking of you. Hope you are having a nice dinner with your family. Gareth x

Billie's heart thundered in her chest. She'd been worried about the fallout with Amber all day and had almost texted him a dozen times but had forced herself not to. Gareth needed to focus on his daughter—this mess was not about her. Not really anyway.

She stared at the screen. Her heart fluttered as she read and re-read '*Thinking of you*'. And that little 'x'. What the hell did that mean?

Her fingers shook as she tapped in a quick response.

Am going mad. Rescue me?

Her thumb hovered over the send button. Should she? Shouldn't she?

'Amber.' Her mother's gentle reprimand pulled all Billie's strings.

That was it. She needed to get out of here and the text left the ball in his court. He could send something flippant and noncommittal or he might just help.

She hit send.

Billie nervously placed the phone on the table, ignoring her mother's pursed lips. Would Gareth come to her rescue?

The phone vibrated almost instantly. She picked it up and swiped her thumb across the screen to read the new message.

Getting in car now. I'll be at yours in twenty. Plead a headache.

Billie smiled. She stood abruptly, cutting her father off in midstream as everyone jumped. 'I'm sorry. I have a headache,' she announced. She grabbed her bag from where it was hanging over the back of her chair. 'I'm going home.'

'That was sudden,' her father, who never liked being interrupted, said waspishly as he half stood.

'No, don't get up,' Billie dismissed, waving him back into his chair. She whipped around the table, doling out kisses. 'I'm fine. Just need to lie down in a dark room.'

With a very hot nurse.

'I'll see everyone next month.'

And before anyone could catch their breath she was practically running out of the house, her fingers flying over her phone keyboard.

See you soon.

She hesitated about putting an 'x' there as he had done. After last night it seemed natural but then, after everything this morning, she wasn't sure…

After dithering for a few seconds Billie decided against it, hitting send exactly as it was as she climbed into her car and reversed in a flurry of gravel down the driveway.

CHAPTER TWENTY

FORTY MINUTES LATER Gareth rolled onto his back in the middle of Billie's hallway, half-clothed, and groaned.

'Well…that was intense…'

Billie, her head still spinning, laughed as she slid her head onto his shoulder. 'Only what you deserved for rescuing a damsel in distress.'

Gareth gave a half-laugh. 'Well…you know what they say…you can take the guy out of the military…'

'Mmm,' Billie murmured, inhaling the smell of his skin, revelling in the warmth of his meaty pectoral muscle against her cheek. 'That blew my mind.'

Gareth shut his eyes as her nuzzling streaked hot arrows to his groin. How was that even *possible* so soon? 'A little on the fast side,' he murmured, thinking about their mad dash from the driveway to the door then collapsing to the floor once they'd got inside.

Billie turned her head until her chin was resting on his chest. Her gaze travelled up his whiskery throat to the downward sweep of his eyelashes. 'I don't know,' she murmured. 'I like it that you couldn't wait to have me. It's good for my ego.'

His smile did funny things to her pulse. A pulse that was barely back to its normal rhythm. He opened his eyes and their gazes locked and the humour she saw dancing in all that blueness bubbled in her heart.

'Trust me, your ego is going to be well and truly pandered to tonight.'

Gareth shifted then, displacing her, sat first before vaulting to his feet, adjusting his clothing as he went. He turned to look down at her. Her skirt was rucked right up, her blouse was half-undone and her breasts had been removed from her bra cups. Her cheeks were flushed and her hair lay in disarray around her head.

'Damn, you're sexy,' he muttered, offering her his hand.

Billie grinned as she took it and before she knew it she wasn't just on her feet but was swept up in his arms.

'I'm going to need directions,' he said.

She wound her arms around his neck as a nice buzz settled into her bones. She nuzzled his throat. 'You are the last man who needs *any* direction,' she sighed.

He chuckled and she could feel it reverberate through his windpipe. 'I mean to your room.'

Billie blushed, feeling foolish. 'Oh, yes…straight ahead, third door on the right.'

Gareth made it to her room in ten seconds, throwing her on the bed. He watched as her breasts bounced enticingly. 'I'm going to use your en suite,' he said. 'When I get back I'm going to be naked. You'd better be too.'

She quirked an eyebrow at him. 'Or what?'

Gareth grinned. She looked so sexy barely dressed, her mouth a little swollen from their passion, a flirty little dare sparkling in her eyes. He shoved his hands on his hips and let his eyes rake over her. 'I may have to spank you.'

Billie's breath hitched. She'd never been into that kind of thing but Gareth made it sound enticing. 'Maybe I'll stay dressed.'

He chuckled. 'Up to you.'

But when he strode out of the en suite she'd pulled the covers down and she was lying in the middle of the bed gloriously naked. It was his turn to quirk an eyebrow.

'I think I'm too squeamish for S and M.'

Gareth laughed at her slightly defensive tone. 'It's too much hard work anyway.'

Billie relaxed. 'I agree. Dinner with my parents was hard enough.' And she reached over and flicked out the light.

There was a desperation to Billie this time. In the hallway it had been all about burning off the tsunami of lust that had swamped them when they'd first laid eyes on each other again. This time, it seemed to Gareth, it was as if she was using it to obliterate everything else.

Dinner *must* have been a bust.

She clung to him in the aftermath and Gareth held her tight. Their breathing slowly returned to normal and eventually he said, 'Tell me about dinner.'

Billie stirred as Gareth's words sunk in. 'Nothing to tell.'

He trailed his fingers up and down her arm. 'I feel like we just had exorcism sex and that somehow it was related to dinner, and you won't spill the beans?'

'It's the same as it always is,' Billie dismissed. 'Tales of surgical glory interspersed with grilling me about what I'm doing. And tonight, for a lovely added extra, we got a graphic discussion on faecal peritonitis. *While we ate.*'

Gareth chuckled. He couldn't help himself. He could only imagine how that had gone down with Billie's volatile constitution.

'It's not funny,' Billie grouched. 'Give me a patient with a complex web of medical conditions any day.'

Gareth's fingers stilled on her arm. Surely Billie understood that being a GP came with its own set of gruesome realities?

'You do know that GPs deal with some fairly grotesque stuff too, right? They see their fair share of hideous wounds and unsightly conditions. The GP is usually the first place people seek help and it can be pretty raw there at the coalface. You'll still have to tell your patients they're dying. And they *will* die, Billie. In fact, you'll be the one there for them and their family right at the end.'

Billie rolled on her stomach and propped her chin on his chest. She shot him a reproachful look. 'Do I look naive to you?'

'No. Definitely not after that thing you just did anyway.' He grinned.

Billie whacked him playfully on the arm. 'Of course I know I'll come across stuff that will turn my stomach. That I'll have to look a patient in the eye and tell them they've only got a certain amount of time to live. I know that. And it'll be awful.'

Billie didn't even want to think about how awful some of those moments were going to be.

'But at least I'll *know* that patient. I'll have a relationship, a rapport with them. It won't be a stranger telling them.'

Gareth picked up a strand of her hair and rubbed the tip with the pads of his fingers. 'And you think that'll make it *easier*?'

'For them, yes. And also for me...I think. It'll never be easy, of course, but one of the hardest things to take about Corey's death was the fact that he died in a roomful of strangers. *I* had to tell his parents he'd died. *Me.* Who didn't know them from a bar of soap. It shouldn't happen like that, Gareth.'

Billie searched his face earnestly—he understood, didn't he? 'How many men have you seen die from combat wounds far away from the people who loved them?'

She watched him as he stared at the strand of her hair he had in his fingers. 'Too many,' he murmured.

'Exactly.' Billie continued. 'People should die with loved ones around them, not strangers. Their relatives shouldn't be told such devastating news by someone who doesn't know them. And I get that that's the way it is in emergency departments and when you're deployed to a war zone. Of course it is. But I don't want to spend the rest of my life imparting bad news to strangers.'

Gareth's gaze cut to Billie as he let the strand of hair drop. 'So don't.'

Billie stared at him. He made it sound so simple. Could she really get out from under twenty-six years of conditioning and manipulation and dare to reach for *her* dream?

'Tell your parents what you want. You're a big girl now. Billie. What's the worst that could happen?'

'A lot of yelling—my father. And tears—my mother. A lot of guilt tripping and subtle threats.'

'Are they going to stop loving you?'

Billie blinked. It had been a lot of years since she'd felt loved by them. She'd felt tolerated and pushed and pressured but love? She was fairly certain her parents were afraid to love too much again.

'They'll stop inviting me to dinner so I guess there'll be an upside,' she joked, her heart not in it.

'But…' he traced her bottom lip with his thumb '…you'll have what you want. You can be what *you* want.'

'You don't understand. I don't do this kind of thing. I'm the good daughter. The peacekeeper. It was hard enough to sell them on emergency medicine. I think my father may well have a heart attack if I tell him I've decided to become a GP. And my mother…'

Billie didn't want to be the one to kill Jessica twice.

'So you're just going to go along with their vision for you? Even if it means you'll be miserable?'

'I won't be miserable,' Billie protested, no idea now why she was defending the thing she didn't want to Gareth. 'I'll just not be one hundred per cent happy. I'll still see a lot of the stuff I like to deal with. A lot of emergency department stuff is GP territory and you know it.'

'Billie.'

She dropped her gaze from his, staring at the strong pulse beating in his throat. She couldn't bear to see the reproach, the disappointment in his eyes. 'You didn't see my mother the night Jess died. She was so gutted. And in those awful months afterwards she looked at me like I was their lifeline.'

Gareth bit back his reply. He wanted to push more. Push her to see she couldn't live someone else's life for them. But he didn't want to be that person. The one who swooped in and tried to fix everything. It could backfire badly and Billie needed to figure it out for herself.

She glanced up at him. 'You think I should tell them to stick it?'

Gareth gave her a half-smile, his fingers sifting through her hair. 'I think…' *I think I have to choose my words very carefully.* 'You have to make the decision that's right for you. And you've got time to do it. You were going to have to do a few years in a hospital anyway before you branched off into GP land, including time in emergency medicine, so none of this is wasted.'

Billie traced her index finger around his mouth, his whiskers tickling. 'Are you always this wise?'

Gareth rubbed his mouth against the pad of her finger. 'I just want you to be happy, Billie. Life's too short to be miserable.'

Billie thought about Corey. And Jess. And Catherine. And Amber staring down a potential death sentence. He was right. It was far too short to be having hypothetical conversations about her career that even she didn't know the answers to when she had a sex god in her bed.

She shifted, crawling on top of him, pushing up into a sitting position, straddling him. 'I know something that makes me happy,' she said, rubbing herself against him.

He sucked in a quick breath clamping his hands on her hips. 'Coincidentally it makes me pretty damn happy too,' he murmured.

Billie smiled. 'Excellent.'

Gareth had to make a mad dash out of Billie's bed the next morning after sleeping through his alarm and dodging her sleepy advances. 'I'll be quick,' she protested, pulling the sheet back to entice him to stay. 'Like in the hallway.'

Gareth chuckled as he covered her up and kissed her hard on the mouth. It was all right for her, she started at eight, which gave her a whole extra hour to get to St Luke's.

'How about I join you in the shower?' she said from the bed as he headed for the en suite.

'I'm locking the door,' he threw over her shoulder. He'd be late for sure if she was in there with him all wet and slippery and determined.

When Gareth stepped out of the en suite the bed was empty and he could smell coffee and toast. His mouth watered and he followed the intoxicating aromas.

His mouth watered a little more as he entered the kitchen to find Billie standing at the bench in a polar fleece dressing gown, her hair swept up on top of her head, licking jam off her fingers.

'Mmm,' he said, reaching her in three easy strides, slipping his arms around her waist and nuzzling her neck. 'Something smells good.'

'The toast,' she said, picking up a slice and shoving it towards his mouth.

Gareth bit into it. Butter and jam melted against his tongue in some kind of orgasmic mix and he grabbed the slice as she let it go. He stepped back from her, moving to her side, his butt coming to rest against the bench, their hips almost touching.

'Coffee's done,' she said, as the toaster popped and she reached for the freshly cooked slices.

Gareth spied the percolator and headed for it as he downed the last large bite. He pulled two mugs off a nearby stand and filled them both. He knew without asking that she took it black with sugar—the same as him. A sugar bowl sat beside the percolator.

He fixed the coffees and passed hers over. He watched as

she took her first sip and gave a happy little sigh. He'd heard that a lot last night and he laughed.

She smiled at him over the rim of the mug and he noticed she had a smear of butter on her top lip. He was just about to lean down and lick it off when a loud knock sounded on the door.

Gareth frowned down at her. 'Do you usually get visitors at six-thirty in the morning?'

Billie shook her head but her eyes held a little twinkle. 'No. I told my other lover to wait until after you'd left.'

He gave her a wry smile as she placed the mug on the bench but he grabbed her and kissed her hard. Pretend lover or not, he wanted her to know who she'd spent the night with.

Billie's head was spinning as she floated to the door, a goofy smile on her face. It was still there when she opened the door seconds later.

Seeing her visitor on the doorstep killed it dead.

'Dad?'

CHAPTER TWENTY-ONE

'HELLO, WILLAMINA.' HER father pecked her on the cheek.

Billie accepted the kiss automatically. 'Oh… Hi. You're here…early…'

'Morning rounds before my theatre list. Like to stay on top of things.'

'Oh…right.'

'Have you got a moment to chat?' he asked, rubbing his hands together vigorously, and Billie noted absently how nippy it was outside.

'Ah…actually…' she said, trying desperately to think of a way to get him to leave. 'I'm running late for work…'

Her father checked his watch and frowned. 'I thought you said you started at eight this morning? Don't worry,' he dismissed in that way of his that wrote off a person's concerns as trivialities. 'This won't take long.'

He indicated that she should let him pass and Billie stepped back out of deference and habit more than anything. 'I feel like you were distracted last night. Pour me a cup of that coffee I can smell and we can talk. You can't afford to be distracted.'

Billie realised suddenly he was charging ahead and she scrambled to get to the kitchen before him but it was too late. By the time she'd followed him in, her father and Gareth were already eyeing each other.

Her father turned to look at her with ice in his eyes. '*This* is your distraction, I take it?'

For the second morning in a row Billie found herself wishing the floor would open up and swallow her. First Gareth's twenty-year-old daughter had sprung them. And now her father.

'Mr Ashworth-Keyes, sir,' Gareth said, coming forward, his hand extended. 'I'm Gareth Stapleton.'

Billie watched her father reluctantly shake Gareth's hand, finally finding her voice. 'Gareth's a...' She glanced at Gareth, who was looking at her with questioning eyes.

How the hell did she explain Gareth to her father, who thought nurses were handmaidens there to serve doctors' needs and fade into the background at all other times? She was too busy fighting the obvious disapproval that there was a man in her apartment distracting her from the hallowed calling of medicine without facing any more judgement.

'We work together in the ER at St Luke's,' she said, suddenly unable to look at the man who'd warmed her bed all night.

Charles crossed his arms across his chest. 'I take it you're some kind of emergency specialist, although...' his brow puckered as he obviously searched his memory banks '... the name's not familiar...'

Gareth glanced at Billie, who had turned pleading eyes on him. Her cheeks were flushed and he knew what she was asking him to do. But he'd been around enough to know that playing it straight was the best policy. If Billie wanted to lie to her father about her own stuff, that was her prerogative. But he wouldn't.

'Actually, sir, I'm a nurse.'

Had Gareth not been in the middle of this awkward conversation he might have found Billie's father's double-take quite comical. But he was.

Charles turned to Billie. 'A nurse? A *male* nurse.'

Gareth almost laughed out loud. The Ashworth-Keyes'

and the Stapletons may have been miles apart in socio-economic status but Charles had just sounded exactly like his own father when Gareth had told him what he was going to do.

Billie scrambled to Gareth's side. 'He's ex-military, Dad. He did several tours to Africa and the Middle East.'

Gareth looked down at Billie. He understood what she was trying to do but he didn't need her to talk him up. He was proud of what he did and he was damn good at it. He couldn't care less what the Charles Ashworth-Keyes' of the world thought. He met men like him all the time. But he did care what Billie thought. And that, apparently, was embarrassment.

Maybe he shouldn't have expected anything too much, given their brief liaison, but he'd never thought she found what he did for a living lacking in any way.

And he wasn't sure he could be with someone who did.

'I should go,' Gareth announced picking up his coffee mug and draining it.

Billie's father clearly thought so too, folding his arms and looking down his imperious nose at Gareth.

'Okay,' Billie said nervously. 'I'll see you out.'

'No.' Gareth shook his head. 'You stay. I'll see you at work.' He turned to her father. 'Nice meeting you, sir.'

Billie watched as Gareth strode out of the kitchen and she desperately wanted to call him back. The door shut firmly behind him and she knew she'd blown it.

But…it was complicated with her father.

The morning sure hadn't ended the way she'd thought it would. Clearly they sucked at mornings. They needed to stick to the nights.

That was if Gareth ever spoke to her again.

'*A male* nurse?'

'Would you prefer it if I'd slept with a female nurse?' Billie asked waspishly.

Her father glared at her. 'Don't get sassy with me, young lady.'

Billie gathered her wits and girded her loins. She so did not want to talk about Gareth. Not when there was so much she didn't know herself. She turned away, busying herself with pouring his coffee.

'I take it he's the reason you suddenly developed a headache last night?'

Billie doubted her father would understand that she'd walked away from many a family dinner with a splitting headache.

'He's a little old for you, isn't he?'

Billie turned and handed him the mug. 'It's really none of your business.'

He scowled at her. 'I'm the one who paid your exorbitant school fees and tutor fees and university and college fees and bought you a car and got you the residency at St Luke's. If you're about to mess it all up then damn right it's my business.'

And here came the guilt trip. 'Gareth has nothing to do with any of that.'

'You can do better than him,' he announced pompously.

Billie gaped at her father. 'Dad…you don't even know him!'

'I know how it's going to look.'

She shook her head wearily, knowing what was about to follow. 'Maybe I don't care how it looks?'

'You will.'

Billie sighed. God help her if her father ever found out Gareth was a single father who drove a twenty-year-old car and didn't even own his own home.

'I keep forgetting what an incredible snob you are.'

Charles gaped at her and even Billie blinked at her audacity to finally give voice to her criticism. It was the first time she'd ever uttered her innermost thoughts.

'It's them and us, Billie.' He looked down at her the way

he looked down on all non-surgeons, like he had some kind of divine right to walk the earth and everyone else deserved his pity. 'It's better for everyone if the status quo is maintained.'

Billie cringed, just listening to his pompous dribble. But she did what Jess had taught her to do when dealing with their father and his *opinions*—take a deep breath and imagine him in the operating theatre dressed only in his underwear and theatre cap.

Billie almost smiled at the thought. 'Plenty of doctors date nurses, Dad, hell, they even marry them, and you know it.'

'Yes, male doctors and female nurses. Not the other way round. If you ever want to be taken seriously as a specialist, you date other specialists. You marry another specialist.'

Suddenly he frowned, his coffee mug halfway to his lips. 'Wait…you're not thinking of marrying this man, are you?'

Oh, good Lord, would this *never* end? 'Dad…I just met Gareth.'

He gave her evasive answer an approving nod—the first time he'd softened since he'd blustered his way into her house and, like Pavlov's dog, she felt herself responding to it. Being the least bright out of her and Jessica, she'd always striven hard for his approval and even more so since she'd announced she wasn't becoming a surgeon.

She really didn't want to ruin the moment by voicing the truth. She had *feelings* for Gareth.

'Good. You don't need this kind of distraction right now. I'll tell you the same thing I tell all my residents, dating and doctoring don't mix. Concentrate on your work until you've settled into your specialty. There's plenty of time for that love nonsense after that.'

Her father put his coffee mug down. 'Right…must dash. I'm pleased we've had this chat.' He patted her on the shoulder. 'You'll see I'm right, Willamina.' He pecked her on the cheek. 'I'll see myself out, you need to get ready for work, don't want to get a reputation for being late. Punctuality is everything.'

And with that he was striding out of the kitchen and disappearing out her front door.

Billie felt too drained from the conversation to move.

Don't want a reputation for being late. Don't want a reputation for dating nurses.

Her father sucked all the joy out of everything.

And now she had to go and face Gareth, *who was angry with her.* And rightly so.

She wished she could blame that one on her father. Only it was all on her. She'd chosen to deny what Gareth did and invalidate it in one fell swoop. Her father may have been the catalyst but she'd made her own bed on that one.

She'd been a coward and had probably ruined everything.

Billie gripped the bench at the thought. She didn't want to ruin it with Gareth.

Please, let me be able to fix it.

Billie hit the ground running as soon as she got to work. She'd glimpsed Gareth briefly and he'd nodded at her politely but that had been the extent of their interaction. She'd fought back disappointment. After the last two nights she'd have expected one of those secret, knowing smiles, a silent communiqué conveying all kinds of sexy messages, like how pleased he was to see her, or how he couldn't wait to get her alone, or he was picturing her naked and screaming his name.

But, then, she only had herself to blame for its absence.

She made a pact with herself to talk to him this morning before their shift was done. To apologise. Although, if he was avoiding her, as she suspected he was, that might be a little difficult.

But she wasn't going to let this fester. No matter what, she *would* talk to Gareth today—even if she had to lock him in the supply cupboard until he heard her out.

* * *

With that course of action decided on, the *last* person Billie expected to be talking to entered the staffroom at lunchtime and introduced herself. 'Hi. I'm Amber.'

'Oh...yes... Hi,' Billie said, pausing, a sandwich halfway to her lips. 'If you're looking for Gareth he's up in Outpatients for a few hours.'

'No. It's you I want. Do you think we could go somewhere and talk?' Amber looked around at the three other occupants of the room. 'It won't take long.'

A knot of nervous tension screwed tight in Billie's stomach as she forced a smile to her face. 'Of course. We can use one of the offices.'

Billie located the nearest empty office and walked in, with Amber close behind. It was small, with enough room for a desk, a chair and a narrow exam table against the wall. She shut the door and turned to face Gareth's daughter, her nervousness increasing now they were alone.

'I'd like to apologise for Sunday morning,' Amber said, looking defiant, as if she was daring Billie to contradict her. 'I was rude and out of line.'

Billie blinked. That she hadn't expected. 'It was a shock,' Billie dismissed. 'Don't worry about it.'

'No. Well...yes, it was a shock...but my mother taught me better manners than that.'

Billie tensed at the mention of Catherine. Where was this going? 'Like I said...it's fine.'

Amber eyed her for long moments. 'Gareth told you about my mother?'

Billie nodded. 'Yes. I'm very sorry for your loss.'

Amber grunted. 'Why do people always think those words help somehow?'

Billie blushed at Amber's belligerence. She felt like she was walking on eggshells. 'I'm sorry...you're right. They don't. Nothing helps.'

Amber eyed her sharply. 'You talking from *actual* experience or just doctor experience?'

Billie almost laughed at Amber's prioritising. Her father would have had apoplexy to hear Amber dismissing her doctoring in preference to real life. 'My sister died when I was fourteen. I know that's not the same as a mother but it was the single most devastating thing that's ever happened to me.'

Gareth's daughter didn't say anything for long moments as she regarded Billie. 'How old was she? What happened?'

'She was sixteen. A car accident. Joy riding with friends.'

Amber's shoulders sagged as her defiance and belligerence dissipated. 'I'm sorry.'

Billie nodded. 'Thank you.'

There were more long moments of silence as Amber obviously mentally recalculated. 'I came to say that I'm pretty sure Gareth is in love with you and…that's been a lot to take in…'

Whoa! Billie blinked. That was a different kind of L word. But conviction rang in Amber's voice and shone in her gaze.

Had Gareth *told* his daughter that?

'But it's been five years since my mother died and Carly… that's my friend…reckons any other guy would have found someone else a long time ago…so I'm trying to be grown up about this but…he said that you were both at different stages of your lives and it struck me that he might be more…into you than you are to him so…I just wanted to say, if you hurt him, you'll have me to answer to.'

Billie couldn't quite believe she was being threatened by a twenty-year-old but her admiration for Amber grew tenfold.

'Amber…Gareth's a wonderful man and I don't want to hurt him. But he's right. There are complications.' She thought back to that morning. 'I'm…trying.'

'Well, try harder,' she said. 'Or let him go now, before you break his heart. I don't want to watch that again.'

Amber's words sliced right to Billie's core. Maybe Amber was right. How could she be any kind of equal partner to

Gareth when she couldn't even stand up for the things she wanted?

Maybe she should end it. Whatever *it* was.

Her pager beeped, she pulled it off the waistband of her scrubs and looked at the screen.

Incoming trauma.

Bile rose in Billie's throat at the mere thought. 'I'm sorry,' she said. 'I have to go.'

Amber nodded. 'Just think about what I said, okay? After all he'd been through he deserves to be happy. He deserves to be with someone who wants to be with him too.'

Billie nodded. Amber was right. The truth sucked.

CHAPTER TWENTY-TWO

GARETH WAS IN the same cubicle with Billie as they attended to the traumatic amputation of a leg. It was bloody and gory, the male patient having lost a lot of blood—most of it over himself. She did well with holding it together but he was probably the only one in the cubicle who really knew how much it cost her.

How much it had to be turning her stomach.

In fact, when it was done and the patient had been whisked to Theatre, she quickly excused herself. His gaze followed her as she disappeared into the staff restrooms and emerged five minutes later looking very pale and shaky, pressing some paper towels to her mouth.

Gareth would bet his last cent she'd just thrown up.

Their eyes met and she gave him a helpless little shrug.

And his simmering anger cranked up another notch. He'd been furious with her that morning, with the way she'd been uncomfortable about telling her father what he did. But part of him understood she was between a rock and a hard place with her old man.

He understood how fraught those relationships could be. And he understood Billie being reluctant to rock the boat and potentially jeopardise her mother's mental health.

But this…

This…pretence was utter madness. How could she even

contemplate not being true to herself over this? This was the rest of her life.

She was hiding behind a mask that was so thin in places it was slowly cracking. And he couldn't stand by and watch it any longer. It had to stop. He didn't want any part of a woman who had to lie and hide her true self from the people who mattered most. Who was okay with living a lie.

Gareth stepped down from the central work station and stalked towards her. He collected her arm on the way past, spinning her around. 'We need to talk,' he muttered.

Billie should have been annoyed at the firm hold Gareth had on her arm but, frankly, she'd been that close to collapsing it felt good to lean into him. 'Where are we going?'

'In here,' Gareth said, opening the door to one of the back examination rooms that was rarely used. He switched on the light and dragged her inside. 'Sit,' he ordered. She looked like she was about to keel over, for crying out loud.

Billie sat gratefully. 'Before you say anything,' she said, eyeing him as he paced, 'I want to apologise for this morning. My father was rude and insulting and—'

'It's fine,' Gareth dismissed. 'He was taken by surprise, just like Amber was.'

Billie blinked. She hadn't expected him to defend her father. 'Amber's twenty. My father doesn't have that excuse.'

'I don't care about that. Well, I do, but I'm not ashamed of what I am. I was more insulted that *you* felt you had to conceal that than anything your father said. I don't want to be your dirty little secret, Billie, but…that's not what this is about.'

A wave of shame washed over Billie, chasing away the last vestiges of her nausea. She had insulted him. This man who had been nothing but supportive and encouraging.

'You have to tell them you can't be an emergency doctor, Billie. You can't keep going on like this.'

Billie blanched at his suggestion. Her father had just found out about Gareth. *One bombshell at a time, please!* She shook her head. 'I don't think that would be very wise.'

'If you don't, you're going to end up here for ever. Throwing up in that loo for ever.'

'I'm fine now,' she dismissed.

Gareth shook his head. 'You're not *fine.*'

'They're not ready to hear it yet.'

Gareth snorted. 'They're never going to be ready, Billie. C'mon…maybe it won't be as bad as you think. Just rip the plaster off, get it over and done with.'

'I've never been a ripper,' she said, shaking her head. 'I'm more an "ease the plaster off bit by bit" girl. And you said it yourself last night. I have to be doing what I'm doing now anyway before I can go down the GP path so why cause a problem before I need to? In a few years I'll face the choice, the *real* choice, and I can upset the applecart then. Why borrow trouble?'

Billie knew it was classic Jess behaviour—tell her parents what they wanted to hear then spring the bad news on them at the last moment. But it had worked for her sister. Jess had gone to her grave with her parents completely unaware of her plans outside medicine.

The perfect daughter, as far as they were concerned.

And now it was she who had to be the perfect daughter.

Gareth shoved his hands on his hips. 'Because I'm worried you *won't* upset the applecart when the moment comes. The longer you put it off the harder it will be, Billie. And why should you *have* to pretend? This is your *family.* You should be able to *be yourself* around your family and expect their support.'

Billie could see the frustration in Gareth's stance, hear it in his voice, but she knew how best to handle her life, not him. 'Look…' She stood, walking over to him, her legs feeling much stronger now. She stopped when he was an arm's length away. 'I appreciate your concern but I've been dealing with my father for a lot of years and I know how to handle him.'

Gareth couldn't believe it. She was really going to suppress what she wanted for a little peace and quiet? 'So you're just going to keep being a...*coward*, like you were this morning when you couldn't even tell your father I was a nurse?'

Heat rushed to Billie's face at his "coward" taunt. 'I prefer to think of it as self-preservation,' she said waspishly.

Gareth raked a hand through his hair. 'Okay, well...that's fine. But I can't do this, Billie.' His hand dropped to his side. 'I don't think we should do this any more.'

Billie frowned, her heart in her mouth. 'This?'

'You and me,' Gareth said. 'I don't want to be around to watch you grow unhappier and unhappier until you self-destruct from the weight of it all.'

Billie's pulse was thundering through her head as the reality of what he was saying sank in. He was ending whatever it was between them before it had even begun.

So much for thinking it was something *she* was going to decide.

She searched his blue gaze for signs of reluctance or disingenuousness. But it was clear and firm.

A flutter of panic swarmed in her stomach. She didn't want it to be over. 'So that's it? Two nights together with the chemistry between us off the charts and you pull the plug?'

Gareth grimaced. He didn't need to be reminded what he was giving up. It hadn't been easy to start this thing with Billie after five years alone and it was frightening how deeply he already felt.

Which was precisely why he needed to get out now.

'All I have as a man is my self-respect, Billie, and I get that by being true to myself. And I want to be with a woman who's also true to herself. I didn't think I'd find another woman I wanted to be with, to share my life with, after Catherine, but then you came along and you made me smile and I felt good and I started to hope...'

His gaze swept over the freckles on the bridge of her nose and the twin glossy pillows of her mouth. He was going to miss that mouth.

'Now you've got to do what you've got to do. That's fine, I can respect that. But I've got to do what's right for me too and that's not being with someone who still lets her parents dictate her life. I think it's best if we get out now before we're in too deep.'

Billie took a step back. He'd been thinking of a future with her? Something small and fragile fluttered in the vicinity of her heart but the grim line of his mouth quashed it. She'd ruined her chances with him by being such a basket case.

'I'll try and roster myself on opposite shifts to you for your remaining time here but it will be inevitable that some shifts will clash. Can I suggest we try and keep things as civil as possible in that eventuality?'

Billie frowned. Did he think she was going to go all me-doctor-you-nurse on him? 'Of…course.'

Gareth hardened his heart to the catch in her voice. He'd seen the collateral damage broken work relationships could inflict and he didn't want either of them to fall prey to that. But he needed to get away from her now before the catch in her voice had him changing his mind and he hauled her into his arms.

'Well…' He stepped to the side. 'I guess I'll see you around, then.'

Billie nodded but didn't bother to turn and face him. The door clicked shut behind her and she groped for the exam bed in front of her, holding onto it for dear life.

That was it. Over before it had truly begun. Her heart ached already.

It didn't improve at all over the next couple of weeks. They worked a few shifts together but, true to his word, Gareth and Billie passed mostly like ships in the night.

Billie knew it was insane to miss him this much after such

a short time together. It wasn't like they had even been *in* a relationship. They'd had two nights together.

That had been it.

But she did miss him.

Lying in bed at night, she craved him. At work, she listened for his voice. She got all fluttery in the chest when he was there and when he walked by she didn't seem to be able to take her eyes off him.

She felt like a teenager mooning over a screen idol.

But she couldn't stop it either and there were times when she swore he found it difficult to drag his eyes off her too.

They may not be together but he was still under her skin. She only hoped the itch wouldn't be permanent.

Another week passed and Billie found herself working a Saturday day shift with Gareth. It was frantically busy so there wasn't any time for idle chit-chat. Not that they indulged in that any more.

Or ever had, for that matter.

As thrilling as it was to work the odd shift with Gareth, the days she did usually ended up being total downers—a case of look, don't touch and the vague feeling that Gareth was judging her for her choices.

She had had one triumph today, though, and she did a little jig as she snapped cubicle eight's curtain back in place, practically running into Gareth as he bowled past.

'Whoa, there,' he said, reaching out his hands to steady her, and Billie was sure they lingered a little longer than necessary.

'You look like you've had a win,' he said, so politely she wanted to scream.

She smiled at him despite his formality. 'I finally diagnosed this obscure skin condition. The patient's been back three times this last week and we finally nailed it. And, best of all, it's totally treatable!'

Gareth sucked in a breath as Billie literally glowed. Her cheeks were pink and her eyes glittered with excitement.

She was so sexy he wanted to kiss her until they both couldn't breathe.

But they had a trauma coming in.

'That's great,' he said, his tone brisk. 'Unfortunately we have a gunshot victim coming in. Head, chest and abdo wounds. GCS nine. ETA seven minutes. Helen wants you in Resus.'

Billie felt everything deflate inside her. *Crap.* Her smile slid right off her face. 'Oh, God, really?'

'Yep. Really.' He paused for a moment and Billie thought he was going to commiserate with her for a second and her pulse fluttered. 'Remember this feeling, Billie. It's not all skin conditions and surgical abdos.'

Gareth felt like an utter bastard as he walked away. But they were in an emergency department, not a dermatology clinic, for crying out loud.

She wanted this? Well, *this* was the reality.

CHAPTER TWENTY-THREE

BILLIE GOT THROUGH the trauma with her usual degree of bluff. It was raw and bloody and the patient died, and the only thing that prevented her from losing her lunch afterwards was the fact she had to sit with the man's wife and tell her.

And all she could hear in her head the whole time was, *Remember this feeling, Billie.*

Remember it? How could she forget it? She *hated* this feeling. But she was trying her best here—surely he could see that?

She knew he didn't owe her anything but at heart Gareth was a compassionate man and she certainly hadn't deserved his condescension.

And she was damn well going to tell him so.

She spied him from the desk, heading out of the department, his backpack slung over his shoulder, and she checked her watch. His shift had finished.

Before she knew what she was doing, she was following him—no time like the present for giving him a piece of her mind.

She caught sight of him as he turned a corner ahead of her and she realised he was heading for the fire escape that led to the rooftop car park. She rounded that corner and stopped abruptly as the sight of Amber and Gareth embracing in the distance greeted her.

Billie fell back, feeling like she was intruding on their

privacy. She couldn't hear what they were saying but Amber laughed at something her father had said and was looking at Gareth like he hung the moon. They hugged again then Gareth slipped his arm around Amber's waist and they entered the fire escape together.

She'd never felt that with her own father.

Never had a moment like that where they'd just laughed and loved and revelled in their family connection. Charles Ashworth-Keyes just wasn't the touchy-feely kind.

She was overwhelmed as she stood and stared at the closing fire-escape door. She wanted that.

She wanted to feel loved.

And she wanted to love back.

She wanted kids to hug and kiss and be there for. She wanted a man who was going to be there for her too. And her children.

And she wanted to feel the exhilaration of solving a complex medical puzzle and improving somebody's life. And she *never* wanted the feeling of dread that the piercing tone of a siren elicited.

And if a woman with a skin condition and a dead gunshot victim had taught her anything today, it had taught her where her strengths lay.

If Gareth had taught her anything, it was time she stood up for that. And she was tired of pretending.

She was pretty sure Jessica would have kicked her up the butt a long time ago.

She pulled her mobile out of her pocket and tapped off a quick text as she returned to the work station and the last few hours of her shift.

Four hours later Billie was parked in her car outside her parents' house, waiting. Gareth had texted to say he'd be here but he was late and she was running out of bravado.

Headlights flashed in her rear-view mirror and she breathed a sigh of relief when they pulled in behind her.

She got out of the car on shaky legs. The shutting of the door seemed loud in a street full of high walls and immaculately groomed lawns.

'Hi,' she said, as Gareth joined her, and he looked so sexy in his jeans and hoody, like the first time they'd met, she wanted to fling herself at him and beg his forgiveness.

But that wasn't why she was here.

'Hi.' He smiled at her and she felt encouraged. 'What's this about, Billie?'

'I'm telling my parents I'm going to study to be a GP and I needed moral support.'

Gareth regarded her seriously for a few moments. The news made him want to leap in the air but he was aware he'd treated her badly that afternoon. He didn't want her doing it because he'd guilted her into it. If she was going to do something so monumental then she needed to do it for the right reasons.

'Are you sure?'

Billie nodded. 'Yes. I realised today that I'm much better at diagnosing skin conditions than I am at treating gunshot victims. That treating Sally Anders gave me a much bigger rush than treating Danny Wauchope. I don't get the rush that people like you thrive on during a full-on resus. And I think you need that, I think you have to be wired that way to survive in that kind of environment.'

A cold wind blew strands of her loose hair across her face and Billie pushed them back. 'I saw you and Amber together near the fire escape this afternoon and I realised I don't have that kind of relationship with my father and that just seemed…sad. And wrong. Do you want more kids, Gareth?'

Gareth blinked at the unexpected question. 'I'd always thought I'd have more kids…yes.'

Billie nodded. Her future was becoming clearer. 'Can you please come with me while I break the news to my parents? I've tried so many times in the past and failed. I need someone there who's in my corner. Who will also call me on it if I chicken out.'

Gareth smiled. 'Okay. But I'm pretty sure your father isn't going to be happy to see me.'

Billie looked at the ground. Even the bitumen in this street was perfect. 'I know I'm putting you in an awkward position,' she said, raising her head.

Gareth waved his hand. 'You think I care about that? I just need you to be certain.'

'I have never been surer of anything.'

'Okay, then.' He smiled, holding out his hand. 'Let's do this.'

Waiting for the door to open was nerve-racking and she thanked her lucky stars for the warmth and calm, anchoring assurance of Gareth's hand at her back. Her mother answered the door with a puzzled expression but ushered them in anyway after Billie had performed a quick introduction. It was clear from her mother's wary gaze that her father had already mentioned Gareth.

Once the token politeness of drinks and offering of chairs—which they both declined—had been dispensed with her father came right to the point. 'What's this all about, Willamina?'

'I'm here to tell you that I'm not going to pursue a career in emergency medicine. I want to be a GP.'

The silence in the room was tense and lengthy.

'General practice!'

Her father made wanting to be a GP sound like wanting to be a prostitute but Billie was done with backing down.

'Yes.'

Her father slammed his heavy crystal glass down on the coffee table. 'No.'

'Dad. It doesn't matter what you—'

'I said no!' he snapped, advancing on her. 'This is the most preposterous thing I have ever heard. He...' Charles pointed his finger at Gareth as he came closer '…is dumbing you down.'

'He has a name,' Billie retorted, as Gareth swiftly stepped in front of her, blocking her father's progress.

'I think we need to calm down,' Gareth said.

Charles glowered at him. 'Don't tell me how to talk to my daughter.'

Gareth did not budge. 'You need to step back, sir.'

'I will do *no such thing*!'

Billie was quaking internally at the confrontation. She had expected her father to be upset, but not like this. There was a film of spittle coating his lips and he'd gone a very startling shade of red.

She shifted closer to Gareth, who wasn't giving an inch. He was staring at her father with absolute chilling authority.

'Step. Back. Sir.'

Her father halted at the ruthless determination in Gareth's eyes.

'Your daughter is trying to tell you something important, sir. You need to listen.'

'Don't presume to tell me about my daughter,' Charles snapped. 'You don't know her.'

Billie watched Gareth's jaw clench. 'I know that Billie's a brilliant doctor. I know she can't bear blood and gore yet she's working in an emergency department to please you when all she wants to be is a GP.'

'She's always been squeamish,' her father dismissed. 'But she never wanted it until you came along.'

Billie shook her head, coming out from behind Gareth. 'That's not true, Dad. I've *always* wanted to be a GP. I was just never brave enough to tell you.'

'But, Billie…how can you do this?'

Her mother, who had been silent up till now, grasped Billie by her forearms. 'Do you think Jess would have wanted you to *squander* the opportunities you've been given? She wanted to be a cardiothoracic surgeon and she didn't get the chance.

And here you are, alive and well and *spitting* on her memory. First this emergency medicine nonsense and now…*a GP?*'

Billie dragged in a ragged breath at her mother's verbal attack. She was torn between the old habit of shutting her mouth and taking it and the sudden rage inside that demanded her parents know the truth and to hell if it destroyed them.

She'd been silent for far too long.

She wrenched out of her mother's grip. 'Jessica *never* wanted to be a surgeon, cardiothoracic or otherwise,' Billie snapped. 'She wanted to be a kindergarten teacher. But she couldn't tell you that so she…'

Billie didn't realise that tears had sprung to her eyes and were falling down her cheeks until Gareth's arm came around her, and even then she just dashed them away and kept going because she knew if she stopped she wouldn't get this off her chest and after ten years it needed saying.

'…she went out drinking and yahooing and staying out late and she drove in fast cars, hoping that you'd disown her so she could do what *she* wanted.'

Her mother gasped but Billie didn't care about her emotional distress for a moment. It just felt so good to finally get it off her chest.

'You're lying,' her mother said, tears tracking down her face now.

'No.' Billie shook her head. 'I'm not. We talked about everything, Mum. *Everything.*'

Her mother sagged on the couch in a dreadful moment of déjà vu. Her father, to his credit, joined her, putting his arm around his wife's shoulders. Billie wished it didn't have to be this way. But she couldn't sacrifice what she wanted any more in the name of her sister.

And she was pretty sure Jessica—the ultimate free spirit—wouldn't have wanted her to either.

'I'm sorry, Mum…Dad. I didn't want you to find out like this. I didn't want to…upset you. But it's the truth.'

They didn't say anything for long moments. 'So you're

just going to throw everything away…all that education and invaluable career advantage?' her father demanded.

'I'm not the kind of doctor you two are,' Billie said, looking down at her confused parents. 'But that doesn't mean my contribution to medicine will be any less important or that you failed. I'm just not interested in the specialty limelight. I'm going to be a damn good GP and that's enough for me. I hope it can eventually be enough for you.'

'And where does *he* fit in?' her father said, nodding his head at Gareth like he was some kind of new species that needed explaining.

'I love him,' Billie said, her heart hammering in her chest as she looked at the man who had turned her whole world upside down.

'He's going to let me be what I need to be, he's going to be the glue that holds me together when I think I can't do it, and one day soon, I hope, he's going to be the father of your grandchildren, who I *will* take time out of work to raise. And you're going to love him too because he's awesome but also because *I* love him and we come as a package from now on.'

Billie held her breath for long moments as Gareth's blue eyes stared back at her. Somewhere deep inside she'd always known she loved him. But him showing up here tonight despite all the stuff she'd put him through had removed her blinkers. All the impossibilities fell by the wayside and they were just a man and a woman who were meant to be together.

'I love you too,' he said, sliding his arm around her.

Billie's heart cracked wide open as she smiled at him. She knew they had a lot to sort out, a lot of *stuff,* and declaring her love for him in front of two people who weren't exactly amenable to the match was a little unorthodox, but it had felt right.

And she'd waited long enough.

Gareth had helped her see so many truths about herself and she didn't want to spend even a second of her life without him in it.

She looked at her parents. 'I want you to meet the man I love,' she said.

Gareth smiled down at Billie, his heart exploding with a wellspring of emotion. In a million years he hadn't expected this outcome.

But in so many ways it was perfect.

He'd been falling in love with her for weeks, not letting himself sink into it completely, not trusting that it could happen twice in his life. But standing here, looking down at her in front of the people who loved her most, he'd never been more certain of anything.

She had shown him it was possible to love again.

He glanced at Billie's parents, who looked like they'd both been struck by lightning. 'Mr and Mrs Ashworth-Keyes, you have my word that I will make Billie happy to the end of her days. I understand that you're more concerned about her career prospects at the moment and hooking up with a man who isn't of the pedigree you'd imagined. But I promise you, I will be her champion, whatever way she wants to jump.'

Billie's heart just about floated right out of her chest. Her parents were clearly still trying to wrap their heads round things but right now she didn't care if they never got it. She'd spent far too long worrying about them and their expectations.

It was time for her.

She glanced at Gareth. 'I love you,' she murmured.

He smiled at her. 'I love you too.'

And right there, in front of her parents, he kissed her. Long and hard. And Billie didn't give a fig what they thought. She wrapped her arms around his neck and kissed him back.

This was her man. Life was short. And she was never letting him go.

* * * * *